FOR a moment she thought of highway-men, and of one coming through the garden door she had left unlocked for Viola. Why had they not foreseen such a danger? She put on her boots and clutched her umbrella, prepared to scream, and wondering if she could reach the garden door and bolt it before the highwayman came through.

Too late! The door creaked slowly outward—she heard more than saw it—and a single flash from a dark lantern zagged about and caught her eye through the ivied lattice-work of the garden-house wall. She blinked and backed away.

The
Elopement

BY

Phyllis Ann Karr

FAWCETT COVENTRY • NEW YORK

THE ELOPEMENT

Published by Fawcett Coventry Books, CBS Educational and Professional Publishing, a division of CBS Inc.

ISBN: 0-449-50293-7

Printed in the United States of America

First Fawcett Coventry printing: June 1982

10 9 8 7 6 5 4 3 2 1

Chapter 1.

"Well," said Miss Alice Markham, "you may say whatever you will of Lord Spottiswood, but Mrs. Beale is every bit as imperturbable as he ever was."

"Suppose Mrs. Beale were walking in the park very early one morning and caught a stray bullet in the brim of her hat from somebody's dueling pistol—just as happened to Cousin Launcelot last summer. Would she simply take it off, as he did—look at the hole just so..." Miss Viola Ayrsford raised her own dark eyebrow at the pantomime bonnet in her slender fingers... "and remark very coolly, 'If that ball was meant for me, I must recommend the marksman apply himself to further practice. If it was not, I must make the same recommendation, for much the same reason'?"

"Phoo! If Lord Spottiswood were to hold old Lady Dunstable's insufferable little lapdog for a few moments, as a special favor, and it were to...to be insufferable all over his second-best dress—just as happened to Mrs. Beale a few weeks ago—would he simply have called for one of the servant's aprons, without ever raising his voice, tied it on as if it were nothing unusual, and then quietly drunk another cup of tea without making the least fuss or to-do about it?"

"I don't think he would put on a servant's apron," Viola began, "but—"

The Honorable Miss Agnes Merriweather, Viola's

dragon, who was over seventy and had been educated on Swift and Steele, finished Viola's sentence in her own old-fashioned style: "But I can see him taking off his breeches to hang 'em by the fire a-drying whilst he sits bare-rumped to drink his twist."

Alice and Viola went into a gale of blushing giggles. "Oh, my dear, dear Miss Merriweather!" Alice choked out at last, wiping her eyes, "I really don't think you ought to be saying such things to us. Why, they trust you to guard our morals, not to—oh, dear!" The giggles burst forth again.

"Humbug!" said Miss Merriweather. "Don't tell me you don't think it often enough. I don't hold with these newfangled notions of watching your tongues, never mind if you wet your dresses down and let the world watch your limbs."

"That's unjust and unkind, ma'am," protested Viola. "You know that *we* have never dampened our gowns. Cousin Launcelot would not have permitted it," she added with a sigh, "nor would Mrs. Beale."

"And whatever would they say," asked Alice, "if they knew what things you stuff our poor young minds with, whilst they're away in the card room?"

Miss Merriweather chuckled. "Them? Not a thing. Bless you, ain't you just been saying they're both on 'em too dignified to do more than raise an eyebrow? Besides, our Launcelot's known me a sight longer than you have, Mistress Viola—I was dandling him on this bony old knee twenty years before you was born—aye, and he knows that much more of the world. Always did have a sharp head on his shoulders for a younker, that 'un, and a deal more respect for his elders than ever you did, miss," said the old woman, though with a twinkle in her eye. "As for your Mrs. Beale, why, if she don't approve of an old lady and a baron's daughter with a line going back unbroke to Duke William's day,

6

let her keep you in her own eye."

This last remark was not quite fair. For the last half of the Season, Mrs. Beale had as frequently taken charge of both young ladies so that Miss Merriweather could enjoy an hour or two of mock gallantry with any complaisant gentleman old or young, as Miss Merriweather had taken charge so that Mrs. Beale could enjoy an hour or two in the card room, where she usually won. But though the old spinster and the young widow got on well enough together on the whole, there were a few things that rankled Miss Merriweather. One was Mrs. Beale's habit of treating all her acquaintance, high and low, virtually the same. Although Miss Merriweather despised toadeaters, she did consider that this youngish relict of an upstart merchant who had died before gaining so much as a city knighthood ought to treat the Eighteenth Lord Merriweather's daughter with somewhat more deference than she probably treated her washerwoman. Still more objectionable—unaccountably, since the old woman rather approved the trait in her own kinsman Spottiswood—was Mrs. Beale's everlasting composure. If the widow had only let out a squeal, now, or at least looked annoyed, when tiresome old Lady Dunstable's pug-dog piddled in her lap, Miss Merriweather could have taken her to her heart as thoroughly as she had taken little Alice.

"But you could not have been dandling Coz Launcelot twenty years before I was born," said Viola after mental calculation. "Eighteen, at most."

Miss Merriweather chuckled again. "Aye, two years is a huge difference at your age, ain't it? Mayhap the difference atween maid and married matron, eh? And at my age, too—mayhap all the difference left atween the dance and the green-growing grave. But in between, my girls, two years makes hardly a blink to folks in their full flush of life."

7

"A flush would have helped me greatly at loo just now." Edward Duncton, Esquire, "Noddy" to his friends and wellwishers, sauntered up to where the trio sat on the periphery of the ballroom. "But it never was my game. Faro, now—a man can lose devilish elegant at that. But the musicians are about to come back, ain't they? Would either of you ladies take it as an insult if I was to ask the other for the next dance?"

"Oh, Noddy, of course we should not," said Viola.

He feigned embarrassment. "Well, ma'am, the truth of it is that I understood your two companions in the question, but now I see I'll have to beg your arm instead, or else bear the name of a curmudgeonly knave."

Miss Merriweather reached up and rapped his knuckles with her folded fan. "You bear that anyhow, my boy, or the name of a slovenly gent-dowd, and that's worse. But you shan't dance with Miss Ayrsford again this evening, or the gossips'll have the pair of you engaged before dawn. Beshrew me, if I didn't have to sit and guard their morals till Beale comes back, I'd dance with you meself; but you'll not dance with my Viola again, sirrah."

"Baffled! One more dance, and I could have persuaded her to fly with me to the Border at last. But *you* guard their morals, ma'am? Wasn't it just the other night you all but ran away with *me* to the Border, Mistress Merriweather, ma'am?"

"Only to save my poor young lamb from your evil schemes, you false conniver."

He bowed and planted an elaborate kiss on the old lady's beringed fingers. "Ah, madam, if you think marriage would reform me to such an extent as that, you do me grievous wrong."

"And you return the compliment, m'boy, if you think being married to me would leave you the time or strength to lead poor lambs astray. But you couldn't

8

marry her fortune, at least—aye, that'd rest safe enough from your designs. Now go bring us all some punch, wicked man, and show you can make yourself useful as well as ugly."

"Cruel madam! If words were blades...or if blades were half as sharp as your words, or however it goes." He bowed again to the ladies and turned to push his way toward the punch bowl.

Viola laughed. "Poor old Noddy! I think he has been threatening to run away with me since he first saw me in my cradle, only to try and flutter Cousin Launcelot a little."

Alice, meanwhile, was holding her fan up to hide her cheeks. Some of Miss Merriweather's tit for tat with Mr. Duncton had made her blush more or less in earnest. This was not only her first London Season, but her first extended visit to any town larger than Wigan. Her father, Captain Markham of the merchantman *Pride of Liverpool,* had ever mistrusted any place except the Country as a safe home for his only child, but he was gone on a two-year voyage, and his father, Sir Toby Markham, who had been knighted for earning the family fortune in trade, had brought his granddaughter up to Town in the interim. Since Alice's mother was dead and her old nurse not at all qualified for a chaperone, Sir Toby had given her his partner's widow, Mrs. Beale. Alice almost worshipped Mrs. Beale, who had actually gained admission for them to Almack's; and she was deeply sensible of her great good fortune in making friends with Miss Ayrsford; nevertheless, even after six weeks, some of the things these noble folk said and did could still shock—not merely titillate—the city knight's granddaughter a little. At such times, she could only repeat to herself: But Mrs. Beale would not even blink.

"Alice!" Viola whispered suddenly in her ear, "I've just had the most famous idea. My cousin and your dragon—if we were to lay our wager which of them could be flustered the first!"

"Eh?" Miss Merriweather craned forward. "What's that you say, miss? I've sharp ears enough for my time o' life, but not for these blessed *sotty voices* of yours. Now, then, mend your manners and let the whole company into your little lampoons and satires. Who was you a-roasting just then? Miss Emma Bracebridge, was it?"

"Oh, I have you there, ma'am," Viola replied gaily. "Nobody was farther from my mind than poor Emmy Bracebridge."

"Don't try to hoodwink your olders and wisers, my girl. I was watching how you ogled that orange turban of hers."

"Then you'd have lost your bet, for my thoughts were otherwhere entirely. I was just proposing to Alice that we measure odds who could be put more easily into a flutter, Cousin Launcelot or Mrs. Beale."

It was Miss Merriweather's turn to find her companion's remarks excruciatingly humorous. "Lord love you, my dear," she said after a moment, wiping her eyes, "but don't ask me to hold *those* stakes for you, or I'll take 'em to my grave before either one on 'em turns a hair."

"Ah, but that's where you're wrong, my dear, dear ma'am." Viola leaned over and took her chaperone's dry, withery hand in her own. "And you are precisely the person we must have to hold our stakes. For we shall *make* them turn a hair, you see—several hairs, before we've done with them, or I have not a twin brother wandering about the Lakes to avoid the Season, like the gullion he is!"

"And how is it you're going to fluster 'em, mistress?" said the old woman with a flick of her fan.

"I'm not sure yet of the details, but it shall be something so outrageous, so...so original that poor Sebastian would be rusticated at once were he to attempt it at Oxon, which of course he never would, being such a Friday-face—but we shall carry it off splendidly."

"Oh, aye? And lose all your prospects, too, for your pains, belike."

"Oh, no, we won't do that," Viola insisted. "For almost no one else need ever know, outside of our own little circle, you see. Or at the worst, we'll only lose the dull old sticks who would not be worth accepting in any event, whilst the lively young men will like us all the better. If they should hear of it, I mean, which naturally they won't, since none of our circle will care to broadcast it."

"'Almost no one' means the whole of London, Mistress Contrary, when it comes to tattle," scolded Miss Merriweather, but her tone was not one tenth so sententious as her words.

"So then our garden of suitors will be nicely weeded, and we shall not need to fear any bores in next Season's crop. Come now, Mistress Merriweather, do say you'll keep the stakes for us, there's a sweet old dear."

"But I have not even agreed to the wager yet," Alice reminded her friend. "Indeed, I'm not quite sure we really ought—"

"Tush!" cried Viola with a wave of her fan. "It's no more than to wager on who will dance with whom, is it?" They had been risking sums of threepence and sixpence on these and similar contingencies for a month; they had gone as high as half a crown on the question of whether and to which suitor the slightly fading belle Miss Starkey would announce her engagement by the end of the Season.

"But I could not afford to stake so much as Mrs. Beale and Lord Spottiswood call for, you know," Alice argued. "Not enough, I'm sure, to make such a very outrageous project worth your trouble."

"Worth *our* trouble, you mean! Dear Alice, you never supposed I'd cut you off from all the fun?"

"But—" said Alice.

"You needn't chance more than ten shillings, dear," Viola rushed on, "and I'll give you any odds you like. I'm that sure of Cousin Launcelot. There! Now you must come to Mrs. Beale's defense, you can do no less."

"It is...it seems stupid," said Alice. "And a little sinful?"

"Sinful? Fiddlesticks!" cried Miss Merriweather, snapping her fan. "What's the younger generation coming to?"

"Seven shillings, then," said Viola. "Or a crown, if you prefer. It's not the money, you know, it's the sport of the thing."

"Well...very well," Alice agreed. "Seven shillings. But there shall be no prank. We'll simply watch and see whatever happens in the regular course of events."

"Gads and zookers!" said Miss Merriweather. "Then why stake your shillings at all? You'll both only get 'em back to the same tune as you risked 'em, and you know what our dear Lord preached about that poor, spiritless servant who naught but buried his talents without venturing 'em nor so much as banking 'em."

"Oh, yes, yes," said Noddy Duncton, returning, with four cups of punch balanced between his fingers, in time to hear the last part of Miss Merriweather's speech. "Outer darkness and all that. Which parable was you talking about? Never mind, they pretty well all end the same, some poor chap goes into the outer darkness. Here, won't you ladies help yourselves before I forget m'self and wave a hand? Devilish hard to carry on a sensible conversation without the use of one's hands."

12

"Aye, the more so for you," said Miss Merriweather, "with more wit in your fingers than your tongue."

"Cruel mistress! And you with your fans to help your own wit. I appeal to you, Sweet-and-twenty—" he turned to the younger ladies, "is 't fair to attack a devoted admirer with a fan when he's only armed with cups of punch?"

"Poor Noddy! We'll relieve you at once. Won't we, ma'am?" Viola winked at her chaperone. "Anyhow, I am wonderfully thirsty. Are not you, Alice?"

"Not that I have ever been able to reconcile the Outer Darkness with the Pit," he went on, as they took their sparkling cups from his hands. "The one sounds so open and boundless—exposed, you know—rather squally. Cold. The other sounds closed in, tight. Like a bucket. Airless. More or less tropical, by all accounts. What do you think, *mesdames?*"

"Perhaps wicked Esquimaux go to the Outer Darkness and wicked Sandwich Islanders to the Pit?" Alice suggested.

"Ingenious, ma'am." He applauded, causing her to smile. "Or possibly vice versa—Esquimaux to the Pit and Sandwichers to the Outer Darkness?"

"Aye, we see all this might be matter of great interest to you, sir, shameless nullifidian you are," said Miss Merriweather. "As for us, we're all looking to wake up in the Other Place, ain't we, girls?" (Alice spread her fan and held it up to her face.)

"If I'm a nullifidian, ma'am, I must have caught it from you," said Noddy. "But come with me and be my love, dear Mistress Merriweather, and Hell itself will not seem Hell with you at my side." He looked toward her lap as if to seize her hands, but her right one was occupied with her fan and her left with her punch, so he shrugged and lifted his own cup to his lips. "Decent drink, this, for sparkle and fruit juice. But what was it raised the subject of money?" he inquired after a sip or two. "A likely winner at Goodwood? New information which one Miss Starkey's to take, Hardbottom or Meyer? Couldn't have been the Funds—who talks business at anyone's ball?"

"Nothing so ordinary as any of that, Noddy." Viola half rose, tugged him partway down, and confided as if whispering in his ear, "We are planning a wager on who can be made to turn the first hair, Alice's Mrs. Beale or our own Lord Spottiswood."

"Three hundred guineas on the Beale," said Noddy at once.

"On that tradesman's widow, you noodle?" cried Miss Merriweather. "Five hundred on Launcelot, and name your odds!"

"Oh, dear," murmured Alice.

"There, you see?" Viola was triumphant. "The fortunes of Mistress Merriweather and Mr. Duncton depend upon us, Alice. You must agree to it now."

"Lord, yes. This is inspired, *mesdames*." Noddy bowed to them. "Fortunes will be won and lost all over London. Pity it didn't come earlier, would've livened the whole Season no end. Don't suppose it'd keep till next year?"

"I don't think I shall have another London Season," Alice mused, more than half to herself.

"No, Noddy, it will not keep for a year, and this is the perfect time for it, right now," said Viola. "And you shall *not* spread the word in any of your clubs and gaming hells, under pain of my most severe displeasure. I don't care how many fortunes it may cost you."

Miss Merriweather chuckled. "Zookers, no, you'll not spread this about. Mum's the word, Duncton. You ain't heard the half on it yet."

"And you'd bet on Mrs. Beale in half your haunts, and on Cousin Launcelot in the other half," Viola am-

14

plified, "so you'd probably end even. No, Noddy, now you've made your wager on Mrs. Beale, I shall bind you to win or lose it all, with no chance of hedging your bets."

"Was that the half of it I hadn't heard?" he asked Miss Merriweather. "I protest it don't seem much of a reason to keep such an idea as this to ourselves."

"Ah, but our little violet's scheming something outrageous to befuss 'em," the old lady explained with a wink. "So we've got to keep it all in the family, so's not to lose her reputation for her."

He turned back to Viola. "Love you, my dear, there won't be any need for *you* to try and outrage 'em. Let this get about, and the whole town'll be doing it for you. Best wager since the sex of the late d'Eon."

"Well," said Miss Merriweather, who could remember the Chevalier d'Eon affair at its height, "but we don't want folk waylaying 'em in the alleys to rip off their clothes, do we now?"

"Of course we do not." Viola rapped his elbow with her fan. "So you see, Noddy, my way will be best, and we must keep everything strictly under the rose. But never fear, you and Miss Merriweather will have very important parts to play, besides holding our stakes, I mean."

"Seven shillings apiece," Alice said softly. "Why, it'll be lost in their own eight hundred guineas."

"You two must mount guard upon the objects of the game," Viola was explaining. "You must set your watches by one another's, and note down to the minute the first agitation either of them shows—raised eyebrows don't count—so there will be no question later. Noddy will keep watch on Cousin Launcelot, of course, being thick as inkle weavers with him already. Miss Merriweather, dear, that leaves you the task of insinuating yourself with Mrs. Beale so as to remain ever

15

at her side, at least until she flusters. You can do that, can't you?"

"Aye, for the pleasure of chinking her armor, I guess I can do it," Miss Merriweather replied with another chuckle.

"Splendid! We must rely upon you wholly. Even if you won't be the most disinterested of judges, precisely, having staked guineas of your own on the outcome... Still, needs must, and of course you'll both swear on your honor. As for Alice and myself, we'll be far too busy making the disturbance to observe our Imperturbables."

Alice murmured with a secret sigh, "I know I shall not be having another London Season."

Chapter 2.

In the card room, meanwhile, Launcelot, Lord Spottiswood and Mrs. Juno Beale were indulging in brag.

It was probably both their favorite game at cards, though neither had ever been heard to profess any marked preference for one pastime over another; and both were excellent players, though hardly braggarts in any common sense.

Lord Spottiswood at thirty-eight had outlasted the designs once hatched on every hand against his bachelorhood. Indeed, more than one young lady had herself rebelled when thrown too much in his path, opposing to her relatives' arguments of his lordship's fortune, position, sobriety, and steadiness the counterargument that life with him would be not unlike life with a platter of yesterday's cold cod. Moreover, although his face was handsome enough, in a way that might have been described as vaguely elfin despite its length, strength, and olive complexion, his black eyebrows had begun early to develop those shaggy peaks at midarch more commonly associated with age, and this, coupled with his height and the breadth of his shoulders, lent his person a forbidding appearance. Noddy Duncton, Agnes Merriweather, and his ward Viola, among other friends and close relations, had suggested that if he were to trim his brows he might not frighten away all the pretty young maids; but his stock reply was that the opinions pretty young maids might hold of him was a matter of complete indifference.

Juno Beale, *née* Knaplock, two years the wife and seven the widow of Mr. Matthew Beale of the firm of Markham and Beale, Bedford Street, could still at twenty-eight have passed for a mature twenty-seven. This evening, however, one might have said she was trying to appear fiftyish. Her pale, heart-shaped face was crowned by a black lace cap perched atop hair dressed in a style that had not been in the mode even when she first adopted it ten years ago, but was simple enough to have seemed not completely out of mode had the locks been silver instead of sorrel; and she wore a perfectly opaque black fichu to supplement the ball-dressmaker's art from bodice to throat. "Damme, Juno," Sir Toby Markham had told her as they set out tonight, "let 'em once or twice get a glimpse of that devilish white bosom o' yours, and see how long you'd stay a widow." To which Mrs. Beale, who had heard that sentiment before, replied that she found both the conversation and the card play better when the gentlemen gave more attention to her mind and less to her bosom.

It had been observed that, when present at the same affair, Lord Spottiswood and Mrs. Beale tended to gravitate toward one another's company; but their behavior was such that only the most diligent of gossips could pretend to make any extraordinary tidbit of the phenomenon. This evening, for example, the viscount and the widow had spent an hour at the same table without exchanging half a dozen words on any topic other than brag.

Three other players sat with them at the round gametable. Lady Maria Dashley was a belle of twenty-six who neither shared Mrs. Beale's preference for a well-covered bosom nor allowed her marriage with the handsome Sir Thomas to interfere with her flirtations. (In justice, no more did the handsome Sir Thomas, who was even now paying remarkably amorous respects to Lady Huntburn in the ballroom.) Captain Conybeare of the Horse Guards was recuperating from a slight wound in the left arm, caught in dueling with a fellow officer, and found dealing cards very "therapeutick." No one quite knew why the Honorable Mr. Jeremy Hastings had addicted himself to a kind of play for which he was obviously and peculiarly unsuited.

At the moment, eleven hundred and sixty guineas reposed in the center of the table, and most of that amount had come from Lord Spottiswood, Mrs. Beale, and Mr. Hastings. Lady Dashley had thrown in her three cards immediately on picking them up and looking at them, and Captain Conybeare had followed her example after a few raises, showing himself well content to gaze at the view her ladyship presented him above the table and squeeze her knee below it—a reckless player among men, his gambling habits tended to moderate commendably when there was a beautiful and complaisant woman next him at the table.

Mr. Hastings kept up doggedly with the betting, but the other two seemed to pay him no more heed than they paid to Lady Dashley and her newest gallant. In effect, the game was between Lord Spottiswood and Mrs. Beale.

"Forty guineas," said his lordship, adding two more rouleaux to the pile, returning Mrs. Beale's latest increase in kind, and bringing the stakes to an even twelve hundred.

"The devil!" muttered Mr. Hastings, pushing another forty yellow boys to the center of the table in order to keep himself even. "She'll *have* t' be content soon, if she ain't a complete bubble."

Mrs. Beale added two rouleaux of the same size, meeting Lord Spottiswood's last bid and raising it in her turn.

Without a pause, he put in sixty guineas.

Mr. Hastings cursed a little more loudly and donated three more rouleaux to protect his stake.

For the first time that hand, Mrs. Beale flicked one of her dispassionate glances at him. "Let us have done with this, I think," she remarked, and put in two twenty-guinea and four fifty-guinea rouleaux.

"To oblige you, madam," said Lord Spottiswood. With no visible sign of either regret or relief, he confined his next and final bet to a simple pair of hundred-guinea rouleaux.

Mr. Hastings imperfectly suppressed a groan, tapped his last three rouleaux, hesitated for a few moments, explored his pockets to make up the sum, and added his two hundred.

Mrs. Beale spread her three cards face up on the table, displaying the two black aces and the knave of clubs.

"The devil!" Mr. Hastings half screamed, jumping to his feet and tearing his cards down the middle in one convulsive movement. Everywhere in the room, players at other tables turned and looked.

But Lord Spottiswood, paying no attention to Hastings's outbreak, observed with the hint of an amused smile, "I came within ambs-ace, however," and spread his own cards to reveal the two red aces and the nine of diamonds.

Captain Conybeare emitted a whistle. "The four aces *and* all three braggers broke up between two hands in the same deal! What's the odds against that, Spottiswood?"

"I have never calculated them, Captain," Spottiswood replied.

"High enough," said Mrs. Beale, "that had I held
your lordship's cards, I should have been tempted to
stake almost as much as upon those I actually held."

"And the pity of it is," Lady Dashley mourned, "the
outcome would have been just the same even if the
braggers were not wild. Why such a pip as an ace should
be wasted as a wild card when—"

"I have been robbed, sharped, cozened, and cheated!"
cried Mr. Hastings.

"Recollect that we are at a friendly ball, sir," said
Lord Spottiswood, "and try to refrain from behavior
more fitting to a hell."

"Even if your verbs applied to the situation," said
Mrs. Beale, "a single one of them would have sufficed."

Conybeare had been piecing together the torn halves
of Hastings's cards. "Why, you chuckle-head, all you
held was two ladies and a king! What was you thinking—"

"Good enough to have won any hand these two
hours," Hastings returned. It was not an accurate statement, but he had clearly passed beyond the constraints
of mere accuracy. Leaning across the table, he seized
Spottiswood's neckcloth. "I demand satisfaction, sir!"

Lady Dashley jumped up with a tiny scream, and
Captain Conybeare grappled Hastings from behind.

Lord Spottiswood remained seated and, except for
his garments, unruffled. "I doubt the table was not
designed to bear both your weight, gentlemen," he observed. "A little more, and you may overturn it. You
have already scattered Mrs. Beale's winnings. Fortunately, I remember the sum."

"So do I," said Mrs. Beale. "But—"

"Aye, I'll wager you do," said Hastings with a growl.
"Unfortunately for you, since it is one bet you would

win," said Spottiswood, "you may encounter difficulty in finding a taker."

The table creaked.

"But do I collect, Mr. Hastings," Mrs. Beale went on, "that you imagine his lordship and myself were acting in collusion to part you from your guineas?"

"And if you wasn't a female, ma'am..." Hastings grunted. "But I'll make him squeal for the both of you, hang me if I don't!"

But it was the table that squealed, not his lordship.

"Damme, it won't hold water!" cried Conybeare, trying to lever his forearm beneath Hastings' chin. "'T was Lady Dashley dealt those cards—you'll have t' call us all out, you madbrain!"

Lord Spottiswood glanced down at Hastings' hand. "Let it be fists and neckcloths at arm's length," he said, without, however, moving a limb. "I apprehend you'll have the more to fear, Hastings. I think I am not considered a dandy, while you, if memory serves, were affecting what I believe is termed a Double Waterfall, though it has now fallen victim to your fury."

"You won't get at me that way, you titled rogue—" Hastings twisted his hand to tighten his hold on Spottiswood's neckcloth whilst thrashing at Conybeare with his other arm, but Conybeare returned the compliment a bit too enthusiastically, and the table overturned at last.

When the echoes of the crash died away, Conybeare and Hastings, the latter still clutching most of Lord Spottiswood's neckcloth, were wrestling amidst the scattered cards, rouleaux, and spilled guineas, Lady Dashley was bending down trying to pommel them with her two small fists, and several gentlemen from other tables were converging to begin the operation of pulling them apart. The table—still, almost miraculously, whole—had landed on its side, presenting its top to the

22

combatants and its legs to Lord Spottiswood and Mrs. Beale. He had been drawn partially up, in accordance with the laws of dynamics, as the table started to turn, but had settled back into his chair when his neckcloth gave way and parted company with the rest of his evening dress. She had remained seated throughout, even when one of the table legs swung up within a few inches of her.

Lord Spottiswood looked at Mrs. Beale and raised his right eyebrow. "Under the circumstances, madam, I trust you will pardon my bare throat."

"I fear you may have sustained rope burns, sir?"

"A few, perhaps, but they should clear quickly. The cloth was a tolerably smooth superfine." He uncrossed his legs, stood, and offered her his arm. Accepting it, she rose in her turn and they stepped forward between the table legs for a closer look at the combat.

The others were just getting Conybeare and Hastings separated, and Lady Dashley was already dabbing her handkerchief at a trickle of blood beneath the captain's nose.

"Mr. Hastings," said Mrs. Beale, "had we—"

"Well, if you wasn't in it together from the first, madam," he shouted at her from the restraining arms of Lord Vieuxbois and Sir Richard Armstead, "you're the coldest, most conniving, heartless, unwomanly minx that ever fuzzed a pack!"

"You are curiously addicted to the use of several words where any one of them alone would have conveyed your thought, Mr. Hastings," she replied. "I suppose you are a poetic soul groping after hyperbole. With such cards as I held, and such cards as I correctly surmised Lord Spottiswood must hold, I could have won double or treble the amount from his lordship, but I allowed pity to take precedence over self-interest, and tried to force you out of a hand I was well aware you

23

could not possibly win. Why did you not throw in your cards at once when I first bet a hundred guineas, Mr. Hastings? Out of tender weakness for you, I cast away a rare chance before half exhausting its possibilities. I was really rather distraught with your persistence in staying where you were so little wanted," she added in a manner that suggested her distraction resembled another person's tranquillity.

"Yes, you block," said Conybeare, "nobody told you to keep flinging your ready away to the winds, y'know. Devil take it, you was always cautious enough whenever *I* had the winning cards!"

"I should warn you, Mr. Hastings," said Lord Spottiswood, who had produced a large black silk handkerchief from his pocket and was now tying it carelessly about his throat in lieu of a neckcloth, "I do not duel. If you send a challenge round in the morning, it will be ignored."

"What, after the way he insulted Mrs. Beale?" cried Lady Dashley, and several of the other guests echoed her sentiment.

Lord Spottiswood cocked his right brow at Mrs. Beale. "Am I anything to you, madam, or you to me, that it should devolve upon me to defend your honor?"

Mrs. Beale cocked her left brow at him. "Not that I am aware of, sir. The various branches of family trees do entangle over the generations, but so far as I know, we are the merest social acquaintance."

He turned to the other guests. "Are you satisfied, *mesdames* and *messieurs?*"

"No, damme, sir," cried Sir Richard. "If you won't stand up for her, I will!"

Lord Spottiswood and Mrs. Beale each lifted a brow at the last speaker.

"Aye, the honor of every lady is at stake," said a

24

gentleman somewhere in the rear ranks of the crowd.

Mrs. Beale looked at Lady Dashley. "Did you feel yourself included in the words Mr. Hastings lately addressed to me?"

Her ladyship looked up from Captain Conybeare's nose. "Let me see, what were they? 'Minx' was amongst 'em, wasn't it? And 'conniving,' and 'hard-hearted'?"

"'Heartless,' to be precise," said Mrs. Beale. "'Cold' and 'unwomanly' complete the catalogue. Well?"

"Why, no, I confess I did not take any of it in a personal sense, not as applying to myself," Lady Dashley admitted under the gaze of Mrs. Beale's brown eyes. "Unless very generally—'unwomanly' as opposed to 'womanly,' you know, and that seems rather a compliment."

"It's the principle of the thing," insisted Sir Richard. "If we let the rascal go away scot-free after insulting one female—"

A rumble of voices, chiefly male, joined in.

Mrs. Beale said, raising her voice just sufficiently to make it heard, and without increasing her rate of speech, "In any case, *messieurs*, it is entirely a matter of opinion whether Mr. Hastings' adjectives were an insult or a compliment. But should any of you gentlemen offer to defend my honor, and thus imply that it requires defense or that I am incapable of guarding it myself, I will regard him and not Mr. Hastings as having offered me the worse insult. Rarely as I take the dance floor, I should prefer that a gentleman stand up *with* me rather than *for* me."

Captain Conybeare removed Lady Dashley's handkerchief-wielding fingers from his upper lip, pressing them tenderly in the process. "Hope you won't object if I call him out on my own score, ma'am. The fellow good as accused me of helping you rook him."

"Aye," muttered Hastings, "as honest a party as in
25

any pack once the kings and queens are out."

"How you settle your own affairs must be a matter of indifference to us," replied Lord Spottiswood, "but I would advise you to have some regard for your host and hostess, if not for the niceties of the *duello,* and wait until morning before you send your friends round to each other. Meanwhile, you might more profitably employ your time in righting the table and bringing Mrs. Beale's winnings around to her. Two thousand and forty was the sum."

Lady Dashley's hand now rested on Captain Conybeare's left arm. Of a sudden he grimaced. "Don't squeeze, ma'am! Damme if that cursed sword cut ain't opened up again."

"In so far as you suffer for having rendered me assistance, even though unsolicited," said Lord Spottiswood with a slight bow, "I offer my commiserations." He turned his head back to Mrs. Beale. "Madam, I see an unoccupied table and a new pack in the far south corner."

She consulted her watch. "And I can play another forty-three minutes before my party expects my return to the ballroom."

With nods to the assemblage, they turned and made their way to the unoccupied table. A number of guests lingered to see the erstwhile battlefield set to rights and the stakes gathered up. Prominent among these were Sir Richard, who offered Captain Conybeare his services as second, and Lord Vieuxbois, who took it on himself to count the 2,040 guineas before delivering them to Mrs. Beale.

Other guests followed the viscount and the widow at once, not to join their new game, but to watch it. Many of these eventually turned away again to their own tables, for watching Lord Spottiswood and Mrs. Beale play at brag was somewhat like watching a pair of oak trees pitted against one another, and the next three quarters of an hour discovered no more such spectacular hands, only a majority of small piles won by the gentleman and a minority of large ones captured by the lady.

A few of the inveterate players, however, who regarded social tables like these as mere stopgaps to make a ball endurable, watched this game to the end. And when at last Mrs. Beale had her winnings, which remained a little over two thousand guineas, changed into bank notes by the obliging Lord Vieuxbois, and quit the card room, these inveterates expressed some private regret that they could not face her in the more important play at their clubs and hells. "A damned waste," one young roué put it at The Brimstone two nights later, "for a female who handles cards like that to throw the rest of her life away in your dratted Straitlacedom." Upon hearing which his doxy, who had not infrequently loaned him cash to cover his losses, boxed him on the ear.

As for Lord Spottiswood, he played at his clubs, and sometimes played deep (though no deeper than the Spottiswood fortune would allow), but the inveterates had long ago relinquished any hope of pitting their wits against his in the hells. For a while after this famous night, however, in the hells as here and there elsewhere, one might glimpse young bloods, otherwise well dressed, who sported black silk handkerchiefs in place of neckcloths, tied with pretentious lack of care in what they called the Spottiswood Fall. It had a short and limited vogue and was never endorsed nor even recognized by his lordship, but a few bucks continued affecting it well into the next Season, claiming it brought them good luck, so long as no genteel widow was playing against them.

* * *

Meanwhile, when the report of that hand reached the ballroom a few moments after the fact, Noddy Duncton and Agnes Merriweather promptly raised their stakes to fifteen hundred apiece at even odds, remarking that in honor of the sum played for by the objects of their bet, they could do no less. "Besides," said Noddy, "it ain't very like either of us will ever be called on to pay off. Little violet, you'll really have t' go it to ruffle them. Sure you won't accept a raised brow?"

"No," said Viola, "because they are forever raising one brow or the other, and you know very well it signifies nothing. It's merely as much as to quiz somebody through a glass. And it won't count if they merely *say* they have been flustered, either, if they haven't *shown* it."

"Of course not," said Alice. Having committed herself to the enterprise, she felt she might as well enter into its spirit. "That might be no more than mere politeness, like—like saying, 'I understand what a lobster must feel,' when you can really have no notion of it at all."

"Right enough," said Noddy. "But you will allow a shout?"

"Oh, yes, a shout would be just the sort of thing to watch for—unless it's merely a holloa over the distance, of course," Viola qualified. "And if either of them should raise *both* brows—at once, mind you—and frown at the same time, I suppose that might count."

"Aye," said Miss Merriweather with a chuckle, "you'd best allow that much, miss. You've work enough cut out for you as 't is."

Chapter 3.

Much later that night, as the first glow of gray was creeping into the eastern sky, Alice and Mrs. Beale sat in the former's bedroom, sipping warm wine and water and talking woman to woman. (Mrs. Beale had a comfortable house of her own in Islington, but for her duties as duenna she had moved into Sir Toby's rather ostentatious mansion in Mayfair.)

Alice treasured these moments and always sipped her wine very slowly, no matter how sleepy she might feel. Tonight for the first time in more than a week her conscience was not quite at ease, because of the wager; but she had wrestled with the problem in the carriage most of the way home, when the two women had curtailed their conversation lest they disturb the snoring grandfather, and she had succeeded in quieting her qualms with the moral reflection that Mrs. Beale was sure to win, as calmly as she had won that hand at brag, and that by assisting in the prank Alice would help set off her chaperone's sterling temper to its most sublime advantage.

"Were there really more than three thousand guineas scattered when the table overtopped, ma'am?" the young woman asked.

"There may have been, including the unwagered piles at the periphery. There were only a few more than two thousand at stake. I am surprised rumor had not already raised the sum to four or five thousand before it reached you, however."

"Two thousand... golden boys, don't they call them?"

"Yellow boys," said Mrs. Beale. "Two thousand and forty, to be exact."

"Oh, ma'am, I'd have been terrified to play for so much! Why, my hand shook that time Viola persuaded me to threepence a point Tuesday fortnight."

"Good," said Mrs. Beale. "Bear in mind, Alice, that I could not possibly have lost that hand, else I should never have played one tenth so deep." She paused to exhale. (Alice wondered if this were a sigh, and if Viola would have counted it as a sign of emotion. On the whole, she thought not. It was merely Mrs. Beale's way of signifying that she was about to say Something Serious in her role of chaperone.) "I fear," the older woman went on, "that I may have provided you a bad example tonight. Threepennies are quite high enough stakes to play for. Any higher, and enjoyment in the game diminishes as one risks losing more."

"Oh, never fear, ma'am! I could never be so fine a player as you, I'd never even attempt it."

Mrs. Beale seemed to ponder for a moment, sipping her wine, before she gave Alice one of the smiles reserved for their private talks. "In fact, I am a rather poor player at brag, very obvious in my style of betting. Had the gentlemen been keener of observation, they would not have plunged so deep once they saw me prepared to do so. I make some allowance for Lord Spottiswood, as with the cards he held he could have done little less, though I fancy he might have suspected he was beat and only felt in a generous mood. But there is no comprehending the recklessness of Mr. Hastings

30

on any other ground than that he is an even worse player than myself and not only does not practice, but does not understand the best theory of the game."

"Well, I shan't ever gamble like Mr. Hastings, I can promise you that. Nor even like you." Alice heaved a sigh. "But do you think they really mean to fight, Mr. Hastings and Captain Conybeare?"

"Not, I trust, until the captain's earlier wound is quite healed. Although they both seem capable of extreme hotheadedness, and since his fellow officer's sword went through his left arm, our gallant captain might judge himself fit for an encounter with pistols at once. I shall tip a wink to Bow Street in the morning."

"Oh," said Alice. "You're not— Then you— But is it quite our business, ma'am? If the gentlemen wish to fight...they're not any connections to us, are they? Ought we—is it in the rules of Town society for us to interfere?"

"Let us hope they are no more than the merest polite acquaintance to us," said Mrs. Beale. "I believe that what the Town calls Good Society generally disapproves of busybodies who interfere with the free right of two gentlemen to attempt letting each other's blood in accordance with some hasty words uttered in a moment of confusion, and I cannot persuade myself that Mr. Hastings would be any great loss to reasoning society, or Captain Conybeare to the army, although either or both of them may possess sterling qualities not apparent on short acquaintance. Nevertheless, however useful in ridding the world of hotbloods, the practice can also endanger unsuspecting passers-by, as we saw lately in the matter of Lord Spottiswood's hat. So until the rules of Town society find official recognition of more weight than either the common law or the precepts of Christianity, I do not think a word to Bow Street out of order."

31

"And you'll send it anonymously, of course?"

"Of course I shall sign my statement. They usually keep these matters confidential, however; and I rather think that, once having been stopped by a runner on the field of honor and haled before the magistrate, our pretty pair will be content to call their business settled and swear themselves free on their own recognizances without pressing it further."

"But won't someone else tip the wink, ma'am? There was a whole roomful of people saw it, and everyone else who heard of it before we'd left the house."

The older woman smiled. "You are arguing round about yourself, Alice. In certain cases it can be commendable to shift one's position in private debate, but one should always be aware of doing it. We need not be surprised if Lord Spottiswood sends word to the authorities, and there's the possibility Mr. Hastings might do so in secret. But I doubt Captain Conybeare would not, considering his record, while Lady Dashley and the bystanders may all cleave to those rules of Town society which you yourself mentioned some speeches ago. It is not a safe practice to leave anything undone because you think someone else will do it, my dear."

"No, no, of course not," said Alice, thinking not nearly so much of Mr. Hastings and Captain Conybeare as of Mr. Duncton's bet with Miss Merriweather, and whatever scheme Viola might be plotting in her bed at this very moment.

They finished their wine, the older woman bade the younger good night with a kiss, and Alice was left alone to think herself into a sleep of extravagant dreams wherein her beloved Mrs. Beale seemed always to be arriving at the last moment with an army of Bow Street runners who carried the dreamer away from strange adventures to stranger jails and, sometimes, threats of impending execution without trial.

She had been dozing by curtained daylight for some while, still grappling with the fragments of her dreams but now aware that they were mere dreams, when Hennings brought her chocolate at half past ten.

"Shall I make up the fire this morning, miss?" the maid inquired.

"What?" Alice was looking at a letter propped between her cup and the silver chocolate pot on the dainty little tray. "Oh, no, Hennings, it seems quite warm enough today."

"As you will, miss." Hennings poured the chocolate, made her curtsey, and left.

Alice snatched the letter. For a moment it had got mixed up in her head with the wink Mrs. Beale meant to tip Bow Street, but now she recognized the superscription as being in Viola's hand. She broke the wafer, unfolded the sheet, and read,

> My Very Dearest A.,
> We must meet at the Earliest Opportunity. I have the most Famous Plan to tell you—I dreamt of nothing else all night. It will Do the Trick to Perfection, or Nothing can, and be the greatest Sport for us! Can you come round today? Miss M. shall Improve her Acquaintance with Mrs. B., whilst we two slip away to Confer Privately in the old lumber room, where no one ever comes, so that we shall be quite Secure from interruption.
> > Yours, &c.,
> > V.
> P.S. Burn this once you have committed it to memory.

There was not much to commit to memory. The substance of the message was already imprinted in Alice's brain, and she did not suppose her friend wished her to memorize the exact words. But was it really necessary to burn the paper?

She looked at her grate, wondering if there was still enough heat in the ashes for her to stir it up herself. But that might look strange after she had expressly told Hennings it was too warm for a fire. If only the day had been rainy instead of sunny! for then Alice would have agreed to a fire in her bedroom.

In tales people were forever twisting papers up and burning them in the candle flame. Alice found the Patent Improved Instantaneous Light Box on her night table, kindled one of the potassium matches by dipping it into the small bottle of sulphuric acid, and held the flame to the twisted letter. Just as one end got nicely ablaze, she realized that she was likely to have a problem, or, at best, an ashy untidiness when the fire reached the end she was holding. With a stifled squeal, she threw off the bedclothes and dashed barefoot across the floor, holding the fiery twist at arm's length. When she got to the fireplace, she found the flame had blown out in the rush of her flight. She left the smoldering paper in the grate, fetched the Patent Light Box, re-kindled the letter, and watched it consumed at last. "Well—" She sighed, using the poker to stir its remains into last night's ashes and cinders. "Next time I'll know better how to do it. At least she didn't ask me to *eat* the beastly thing!"

"You will see her at Lady Fencourt's this evening, will you not?" said Mrs. Beale when Alice suggested they pay their respects at Ayrsford House after breakfast.

"Yes," said Alice with only the slightest hesitation, "but we must...confer about our dresses."

"Ah, of course." Mrs. Beale went to the ormolu writing desk that had been crowded into one corner of the breakfast room, which, like most of Sir Toby's rooms, tended to be overfurnished.

"And then, you know," Alice added, "when there's dancing, we can't ever feel quite secure just to sit and coze for ten minutes together."

"Nor should you, at your age." Mrs. Beale dipped pen into ink-glass. "If you were not liable to be solicited for at least four dances in six, that would be matter for concern."

Alice did not mention that she and Viola had sat out four dances only last night, by their own choice, to buzz with Miss Merriweather and Mr. Duncton about the conditions of the wager, or, as the younger ladies liked to call it, the Enterprise. "What are you writing, ma'am? The letter to Bow Street?"

"No, I posted that before breakfast. This time I am writing twenty-five...no, twenty-six words to a friend, including the signature." Mrs. Beale sanded the note.

"Oh, dear! You had other plans, and now— Oh, no, ma'am, if you must cancel some plans of your own..."

"Dismiss it from your mind, my dear," said Mrs. Beale in the shade of voice that might have been something between a polite request and a command. "I had thought that a visit to the British Museum might provide us some refreshment from the comparative frivolity of our social duties, and had arranged for a gentleman scholar to show us the finer points of certain antiquities. But I'm sure he will have an equally interesting tour of study without us." She folded the sheet and looked at her charge with one of those smiles that seemed to communicate something of her own inner tranquillity. "It will be of more immediate importance to your grandfather that you and Miss Ayrsford preconcert your attire so as to appear complemental rather than clashing blossoms tonight."

Alice, tranquillized, nodded and refilled her coffee cup.

Mrs. Beale wafered the note and rose. "I'll arrange for the carriage, fetch my workbasket, and be with you again presently." She might have rung for a servant and issued all necessary commands over her second cup of coffee, but she believed that people should not rely utterly upon the demands of leisure to keep their bodies exercised. At home in Islington she kept only a butler, a cook, one footman, a kitchenmaid, and a housemaid who also served, at Mrs. Beale's rare need, as abigail, besides the gardener and one stableman who could double as coachman; and she had been known to make her own jams, wines, and beer, like a country housemistress.

Lord Spottiswood had spent the morning in the British Museum with the Cottonian Manuscripts, to which he had had admission for some years. Henshawe, one of Sir Toby Markham's numerous footmen, found him as he emerged into one of the more public galleries and delivered the note which he had been instructed to put direct into his lordship's hand.

Spottiswood broke the wafer and read:

> Calcutta House, Mayfair
> My Lord,
> I regret that a sudden demand on my afternoon will again prevent our meeting; but youth must sometimes be served.
>
> Beale

He nodded without raising a brow, took a pencil from his pocket, wrote: "Understood. Spottiswood" at the bottom of the sheet, folded it in another fashion with the ends tucked in to supply the lack of a fresh wafer, gave it back and told Henshawe to be sure it reached the lady's hand who had sent it. He then took solitary refreshment in the nearest tea garden, after which he returned to the Museum to spend some hours gazing at the Towneley marbles.

Meanwhile, Alice and Mrs. Beale were driven round to Ayrsford House in Sir Toby's barouche. Alice had never driven any conveyance larger than the little tim-whiskey they kept at home for short visits to country neighbors and shopping trips to Wigan. Mrs. Beale could very well have driven the phaeton or her own landaulet, and an open carriage would have suited the day rather better; but it suited Sir Toby's consequence better to send them in the large new carriage with a liveried coachman on the box and the Markham coat of arms painted brightly on both doors.

The reaction of at least one Ayrsford House inhabitant was not what Sir Toby might have wished. Miss Merriweather glanced out the window at the barouche and asked the visitors who had dismounted therefrom, "Ever rid by chair?"

"Once or twice, when I was younger and newly come up to Town," said Mrs. Beale. "I was not overfavorably impressed."

"Wasn't you, indeed? Only decent way to get about in the streets, ma'am. A good pair o' chairmen, and they'll carry you smooth as sherry over the cobbles, none of this tooth-rattling with the wheels ajouncing on every chip of brick. Yes, I mind when the chairs was thick as penny ballads in Town. That was when folks knew how to travel the streets, aye, and how to put a good scandal into rhyme."

"I think you exaggerate the horrors of travel by carriage," said Mrs. Beale. "When the wheels are well rimmed and the body well hung, not even cobblestones need necessarily crack one's teeth in one's jaw. And, as I recall, one of the chairmen who once carried me had rather a severe limp. As for penny ballads, I have read a few, and I hope you don't pretend they were passable poetry."

" 'T was the tales," said Miss Merriweather, visibly nettled. "A good murder or elopement or hanging done up in rhyme—now there was somewhat to liven the blood. Lord Wyndmont's murder, that was one of the last of the grand, gory ones," she added, smacking her lips.

"I see. The rattling one's teeth did not receive from riding in a sedan chair they did receive from the sorry verse of the ballad mongers."

"Why, ma'am," said Miss Merriweather in disgust, "I doubt you'd call Mother Goose herself a bad poet."

"I would not. Some of the lyrics attributed to that author have a soothing rhythm and an unstrained simplicity too often lacking in the ragged verses of the ballad mongers, as also of certain modern poets with greater pretension to literary merit."

Viola tugged Alice's sleeve. "Come, we'll escape whilst they're at this." More loudly, she said, "We'll just run up to my room now, ma'am, so that I can show Alice those ball dresses I haven't been able to choose between."

"Aye, aye, run along, my girls," said Miss Merriweather. "Precious little harm they can get into together, your chick and mine, eh, ma'am?"

"It seems improbable," said Mrs. Beale. "One is safest, however, to discount no possibility."

That was the last statement Alice could catch as Viola drew her upstairs. "Oh, dear, you don't think she may suspect?" whispered the country girl.

"Of course not, however could she? You didn't let anything slip, did you?"

Alice shook her head.

"So there you have it," Viola pronounced cheerfully. "Here." Pulling her friend past her own bedroom door, she opened another across the passage, motioned Alice in with a bow, followed her, and closed the door on their conference. "Now," she went on, "we are quite safe, provided we don't speak too loudly."

"Ought we not whisper?" Alice whispered.

"My dear, no. They'll think it very odd downstairs not to hear us at all, and when you're downstairs you can't ever be quite sure precisely which room voices are coming from upstairs. I've lived in this house the better part of my life, you know, whenever we're in Town, that is."

"But this is a gentleman's dressing room!" said Alice, staring around. "I thought we were going to the lumber room?"

Viola waved it off. "That was simply a ruse, in case my note fell into the wrong hands." She leaned forward and murmured in her friend's ear, "This is Sebastian's room, you see."

"Your brother's room!"

"Shh! They should hear our voices, but they must not hear what we say. Yes, it's Basty's room, so you see there's no worry. He's not to be in Town for another fortnight, if then, and nobody comes in here except a maid once every few days to keep it aired."

"Oh," said Alice.

"And she was just in yesterday, so there's not the least chance she'll catch us here today. Now!" Viola opened the clothespress, pulled forth a dark green coat, held it up to her bosom, twirled round on her heel, and made Alice a bow, animating the right coat sleeve from without.

"Viola, what..."

"Well, what do you think of my new clothes? It's quite true that I need you to help me make my choice." Viola produced a brown coat from the press and held it up beside the green. "Only these are the two garments I can't choose between. The brown's a bit sober, even for Sebastian, and the least likely of all to draw any second glances. But I'm not entirely sure we want to avoid second glances, and I do like the green, it's the most nearly rakish thing in Basty's whole wardrobe, except the Hessians Uncle Charles gave him last Christmas."

"But, Vi, what do you mean to do with it?"

"Can't you guess?" Viola winked. "We're enough of a size that I can wear my brother's clothes very nicely. I slipped in here last night and tried them on to be sure. Alice, I am going to elope with you to Gretna Green."

Alice put her palm to her cheek and sat down on the nearest chair. "Oh, Viola!"

"It will be perfect. Basty and I look just enough alike that someone who glimpses me from a distance, or who is only acquainted with us in passing, may even mistake me for him! Not that it will be necessary, of course. All anyone need guess is that you're running away with a young man. It may be all to the better if no one suspects who the young man is. But if it *should* be thought for a while that poor, staid old Sebastian is actually doing anything so wicked—oh, what a glorious joke on him!"

"But...but what will they think when they find you're missing, too?"

"I shall leave a note saying I've had a letter from you Revealing All and I've gone at once to find you and companion you for the sake of a little propriety. And I'll hint at the Boroughbridge road, but really we'll go by way of Manchester. That should drag a proper red herring across our trail and give us time for a capital start. We may even make Longtown and wait for them in comfort just this side of the Border. *Kearsley's Guide* recommends the Graham Arms."

"But won't they think it odd that you should have chased off after us at once without going to your guardian and taking him the news first?"

"Let them think it odd! That's precisely what we want 'em to think, and the odder the better. I only wish we could find some way to guarantee my cousin and your dragon might receive the news at exactly the same moment, or otherwise Mrs. Beale is very likely to find you missing before Miss Merriweather is on hand to judge her reaction, and then she'll have time to recover from her first shock. But I suppose we may allow her that equalization."

"Mrs. Beale will not need any equalization," said Alice.

"Well, then, we'll also discount any emotion Cousin Launcelot may show in the first moment of discovery, and only begin the bet from the moment Miss Merriweather is at Mrs. Beale's side and dear old Noddy at my guardian's. That part we can leave to them. They've much more of the ready at stake, after all, and meanwhile we'll be having the lion's share of the fun. But perhaps, if you left word the night before that you were not to be woke until noon, and I were to do the same here, and then Miss Merriweather were to drive round and pay an early call at Calcutta House at half past eleven and Noddy were to be here at the same hour with Cousin Launcelot?"

"Yes," said Alice, "I suppose that would do it...you'll have to arrange it all, though, with Miss Merriweather and Mr. Duncton, I mean."

"And yet I don't know. If our Imperturbables were

41

to crumble at the first shock, there would go our chance of adventure, pop! So it might be best to give them both ten minutes' grace or so to recover from finding us gone."

Alice sighed. "If it's to be our adventure first and foremost, why...But hadn't we best just leave it to Miss Merriweather and Mr. Duncton when they want to start their bet, as you said a moment ago?"

"Yes, you're right. We shouldn't try to dictate their part of the fun, and I daresay they'll be as eager as we are not to cut the chase short before it's half begun. Besides, we'll already be well on our way, and they'll have to catch us up in any event, if only to tell us the wager's won."

"When is it to be?" Alice asked in a voice of resignation.

"Friday night, after the opera. It'll be too long a performance for us to go anywhere else of consequence afterwards, except supper, and yet we'll be at home earlier than when we've been to balls and drums and such, so we'll have more of the night."

"But won't they think it odd we should sleep late after going up to bed earlier than usual?"

"Oh, you Country Dear!" said Viola. "Tell them you don't feel well, then. Powder your face to look a little pale. No one will question it if you're a bit worn out and low this near the end of the Season, especially when you've so often been up betimes as if you were still at home in Lancashire. As for me, I've kept my bed until at least twelve or one most days, whether Jones brings my chocolate at eleven or not. It's a trick Miss Merriweather taught me for staying at one's best during the Season. I read when I can't sleep any longer. I got back into bed this very morning immediately after slipping my letter in the post—oh, it was delicious, nipping out secretly in the early dawn, all alone. It filled me with

42

such confidence, when I was back again safe in my own room with the mission successful, that I feel ready for any adventure."

"I suppose I ought to try something of the sort, then," said Alice with another sigh. "I made rather a bungle of burning your letter."

"Never fret. I've confidence for us both. Well, you've but to write your note—we have two days to settle exactly what you'll say in it—pack up your portmanteau, and wait for me at Calcutta House. I'll take care of all the rest. I'm the young man, you know. Cousin Launcelot was so generous at Christmas that I still have most of the pin money he's supplied me since," said Viola, who had also learned from her duenna the female prudence of keeping a secret store of ready cash, "and Miss Merriweather and Mr. Duncton will give us more, so there's no need to worry ourselves there—and what a great joke that Cousin Launcelot will have provided so much of the capital himself, all unknowing! So you needn't even bring along any pocket money, though you may if you like, of course."

"What sort of things ought I pack?"

"Oh, whatever you'd take if it were a real flight to Gretna Green, you know."

"No, I don't. I've never eloped before."

"Whatever you'd need for a fortnight's stay anywhere."

"Carruthers has always done my packing for me whenever I went anywhere at all," said Alice. "And this summer is the first really long visit I've made farther than Lancashire, and I've always visited relations who could lend me anything I needed and didn't have with me."

"Well, I'm afraid you can't leave it to Carruthers this time. I have decided we must have no abigails nor footmen nor any attendants at all. We'll get on much better

43

without servants. Either they'd be trying to stop us, or talk us out of it, or blabbing, or if they should fall in with a good heart, we'd only get them into a rather nasty kettle of fish. Our families shan't be able to do anything to us afterwards, worse than a scold, I mean, or a few days without dinner, and it'll have been worth that. But they might turn any attendants who had helped us out of doors without a character."

If Alice thought that Sir Toby, Mrs. Beale, and especially Captain Markham when he finally came home again from sea might find some considerably worse chastisement for her than a scold and a few days without dinner, she kept that fear to herself. "Yes, I understand about the servants, but what am I to pack?"

"Surely you know what you use once it's unpacked wherever you're visiting? Well, never mind. I'll draw up a list and you can look it over." Viola giggled. "And you need not bring along any gauzy silks or cobweb lawn or any of those special little fal-lals and folderols for the wedding night and the honeymoon, you know."

"I don't think I even have anything like that. Will I need to climb down a ladder from my window?"

"I hope not," said Viola. "I shan't be able to bring one along in the cabriolet, and it would be risky to rely upon finding one about the premises. Try to slip down the back stairs. If it's a clear night you can wait in the garden. If it rains, wait for my signal at your bedroom window. Would you rather I whistled, or threw a pebble, or flashed a dark lantern?"

"I think I'd rather wait in the gardenhouse. The noise or the light might call someone's attention to us."

"Oh, excellent! You see, you can use your head, when you put your mind to it." Viola paused a moment, cocking her own head as if to reexamine her last sentence. Then she laughed and shrugged. "So now, which shall it be, the green coat or the brown?"

"Hadn't we better decide what gowns we'll wear to Lady Fencourt's tonight, since that's what they think downstairs we're doing?"

"It's only what Mrs. Beale thinks," said Viola with a wide smile. "Miss Merriweather knows what we're really about, more or less. But you're quite right, and I'm more and more glad to have your mind along, now we've wound it up. Don't you have a nice cream-colored gown you've hardly worn?"

Alice nodded.

"Good. Then I'll wear my cranberry-colored one. Now that's settled, milady, will you have your gallant a greencoat or a brown?"

"Perhaps you'd best take both," said Alice, "if we're to be gone a fortnight."

Henshawe put the twice-folded note on a silver tray and presented it to Mrs. Beale that afternoon when she and Alice had returned to Sir Toby's house and were resting for a few moments in the parlor.

Mrs. Beale unfolded the sheet and read his lordship's penciled addition. "Excellent scansion," she murmured. "Rhyme, also."

"What is it, ma'am?" asked Alice.

"Only a short response from the gentleman scholar who was to have shown us the Towneley marbles," said Mrs. Beale. "There will be no answer, Henshawe."

When the footman had left, Mrs. Beale went on mildly, "You would not read letters meant for other people, Alice. Neither is it the best form to question them about the contents."

"Yes, ma'am," said Alice.

Mrs. Beale crumpled the paper into a neat ball. A very close observer might have suspected an extremely slight mistiness about her eyes. But Alice was not a close observer, for she was diligently trying to put all curiosity out of her mind (and succeeding pretty well, thanks to her own preoccupation).

"It is time to dress for dinner," said Mrs. Beale.

"Yes, ma'am," Alice concurred, and departed for her dressing room.

Mrs. Beale dropped the crumpled note onto the grate and watched the heat momentarily illume some letters of the message, "Understood. Spottiswood," before the paper blackened into the likeness of another, though more fragile, lump of coal. "Excellent rhyme and scansion," she repeated to herself. "Coincidental, of course." Then, because the episode was, after all, of minute importance in the design of the universe, she left the parlor for her own dressing room.

Chapter 4.

In fact, neither Mrs. Beale's message to Bow Street, nor a call which Lord Spottiswood had paid at the same address before proceeding to the British Museum had any effect on the affair between Captain Conybeare and Mr. Hastings. The runners might undertake to keep watch for the duel, but their vigilance was unnecessary, thanks to Conybeare's choice of a second.

August Modrowski, count and patriot of a nation divided amongst her enemies within his own memory, had taken part as a boy of fourteen in Kosciuszko's half-year uprising. Badly wounded in the fatal battle of Maciejowice, he had been saved by loyal peasants, faithful friends, and the fact that his injuries rendered him—unconscious for much of the time—unable to step forward and declare his involvement to the world. As the Third Partition wiped his native Poland from the political map of Europe, the young nobleman was spirited away to the refuge community in Paris, where as soon as the chance arose he joined Bonaparte's army as an officer in General Dabrowski's Polish Legions. He served the Corsican ardently until at last, during the Spanish campaign, he fell a wounded prisoner to Lieutenant James Standeven of the Royal Horse Guards.

Standeven was an officer and a gentleman, Modrowski a gentleman and an officer. Mutual admiration for the enemy's gallantry ripened almost at once into fast friendship between captor and prisoner, the more so as neither considered England and Poland "natural enemies," as were, for example, England and France, or Poland and Prussia. Both could speak French, but they had given each other a few first lessons in their respective native tongues, and had Bonaparte's establishment of the Duchy of Warsaw a few years earlier not rekindled the Polander's zeal for active service, the Briton might have persuaded him to give his parole even before seeing him shipped to England, already more of a convalescent than a captive.

The news that arrived a few months later of Standeven's death in action completed the work of his persuasive efforts, and in memory of his friend, the romantic Polish count pledged his word neither to attempt escape nor ever again to take up arms against Britannia. Some captured French officers were weekly reconciling attempts to escape England with their oaths to remain, but Modrowski would have regarded his parole as more sacred than that, even if his own land of birth had lain just across the Channel. He quartered in London and spent much of his time perfecting his English in the daily society of British officers and the not infrequent society of nonmilitary gentlemen and ladies.

On the whole, he did not find English ladies as beautiful as his own countrywomen, but, being far too gallant to hint as much to them, became something of a favorite at each gathering he attended. His various wounds old and new had left his lean, handsome face intact save for a tiny scar on the right cheek where a bullet had brushed it at the glorious Battle of Raclawice, while the slight stiffness in his left arm and the stitch in his ribs which occasionally troubled him after

48

one fast country dance too many added to his attractiveness. It was, however, the wives, the widows, and the shelved but still flirtatious dames who fluttered round him most. The serious husband-seekers (or, perhaps more to the point, their parents and guardians) tended to strike off a foreign prisoner of war whose rightful patrimony was not only located in central Europe but rendered dubious by the political situation.

So he spent two winters and a summer. Then, one evening early in the second summer, he sat down to cards with Captain Conybeare of the Horse Guards.

A few nights earlier, Conybeare had won Bluebriar, an estate in Northumberland, from His Grace the Duke of Exe. Although a fine old house with several choice hides of land yielding annual rents that would have seemed a good income to anyone whose fortune was less than the duke's, Bluebriar was so remote both from London and from his other properties that His Grace wrote the loss off with a shrug. On losing Bluebriar in his turn to Modrowski, whose luck was remarkably good that week, Conybeare imitiated the duke's shrug and called for another bottle of hock. He had had similar windfalls and reverses before now.

Fortunately for himself, however, Count Modrowski was a social rather than an inveterate gambler, notwithstanding his most profitable run of fortune. As long as he had had pay commensurate with his rank, paid him more regularly as a captured officer by the British than it had been by the French when he was in free and active service, and nothing to spend it on but his personal daily needs, he could afford to plunge as deeply as his previously amassed winnings would allow. All that changed when the deed to a good property opened up new choices to him. At once he stopped playing for any stakes higher than a few guineas.

He considered that his parole must hinder any future

usefulness of his to *l'Empereur* until such time as Britain changed from an enemy to an ally of Bonaparte; that such a shift seemed improbable within the next ten or twenty years; that from what he had seen of the Celts they were as tenacious as the Poles, so that until they did come over to Bonaparte's Grand Design, thus helping assure its eventual success, his own ancestral lands were likely to remain inaccessible to him; and that the hero Kosciuszko himself had expressed doubts of *l'Empereur*'s sincerity. The count therefore penned his resignation from the French army, virtually changing his status from prisoner of war to emigrant, and began preparations for a trip north to look at his property, with the view of taking up life as a country gentleman in his adopted land.

On the eve of Modrowski's departure, Conybeare's affair with Hastings arose. Conybeare, thinking no less of the Polish count for the latter's retirement from the gaming tables, solicited him as a second. Modrowski obligingly put off his journey for a few days, reread the *Code Duello,* and went around to see Mr. Hastings's second.

This person proved to be a fire-eater of the most enthusiastic description. "My principal," said he, "demands satisfaction from *somebody,* and if he can't get it from Spottiswood, damned if we don't take it out of Conybeare's hide."

"Nevertheless, Captain Conybeare was not involved directly. By chance, he was at the same table. That is all."

"All the less right to meddle in the business. Not involved, you say? Dashers, man, there was blows given."

"This 'dashers,'" said Modrowski. "You use it for an oath, like 'the devil,' or is it the name for a blow, or do you insult the ladies who were there present?"

"By God," growled the other, doubling his fists, "if you're making light of my oaths, you furriner..."

Modrowski controlled his not inconsiderable temper and spread his palms. "I simply asked to learn the language. As for blows, my principal simply held yours so there were no blows."

"Hah! So he told you, I guess."

"The table fell, did it not? Your man perhaps thought there were blows then, and it was not his fault to think it. But if there was blows given, they was given by both men."

"There's no forgiving blows. Not without an exchange of shots, there ain't. And if your man got some as well as gave, he'll be all the more eager for a go at mine. If he's a man of honor, that is."

Modrowski reflected that, whereas his principal might be eager for the fight, Northumberland and Bluebriar were calling himself. "There were women involved, and I think they were not 'dashers.' Much can be forgiven, if it is done for the honor of a woman. Even to blows."

"Dashers, the females make it worse. There's their honor at stake, too, you blasted frog."

"I am not a 'frog.' I am a Pole. Nor are the Hollanders 'frogs,' neither," Modrowski added. "Frogs are little green animals, *żaby* we call them in Polish."

"Slimy little green animals that croak and puff 'emselves up and then hop away, like any so-called man as is afraid to stand and fight like a man."

Modrowski turned away from the other second and walked the length of the room, rubbing his chin. His fist ached to smash into the man's face; he could very easily find himself standing across from this *dran* at right angles with the principals, fighting his own secondary duel. But dueling was against the English law, and it occurred to him, a little late, that his own po-

51

sition before that law might be doubly doubtful if he were caught in the act. He did not want to risk it now, when he had property in this land and no place any longer in the French army. Conybeare would have understood this. (Modrowski could not think that even a casual friend might have endangered a companion in simple, unmeditating carlessness.) Therefore, his principal meant him to settle this matter before it reached the dueling ground.

"It is your man who insulted the ladies. You do not deny this?" he asked, turning back.

"Nay. The doxies deserved it."

Modrowski managed to swallow down this insult to ladies with whom he was unacquainted. "You was not there. And if they did or did not, nevertheless my principal acted to defend them."

"Aye, and himself as well—"

"So we may demand the apology. But we do not. We will consider it enough for you to withdraw."

"Eh, you will, will you? Damned good of you and that lily-livered Conybeare of yours. And if my man don't accept?"

"I want to hear it from himself."

The other second spluttered for a moment, substantiating Modrowski's guess that this man was thirstier for blood than his principal. "Ain't done," he said at last. "You'll have t' do all your palavering with me, and that's damn well the long and short of it."

"Mr. Hastings has engaged you because you will make it sure that he fights," said Modrowski.

The other man looked flattered. "Well, I ain't lost my principal his chance yet."

"Then the good Mr. Hastings might as eagerly not fight, but he seeks to...throw away the scabbard. Is it not?"

"Are you—"

"My man sent the challenge," Modrowski said with a smile. "Your man gave him great provocation, but nevertheless my man wrote the letter. So your man needs just to refuse it."

"And be branded a lily-livered coward!"

Modrowski drew off his right glove. "Very brave men have refused the challenge."

"That's not here nor there! Dashers, you frog, when it's a clear case of cheating at play—"

"It is not a clear case. Your man did not send to mine the challenge for cheating. Mine sent yours the challenge for accusing him with no reason." Modrowski drew off his other glove. "*Voici.* I am called a brave man. My body is scarred for my country and for *l'Empereur.* So I am at liberty to ignore any man's cartel, and if one calls me coward, I will show them my scars, *n'est-ce pas?*"

"Here, what—" the other began, starting to back away.

He did not back fast enough. Modrowski's fist caught him square on the chin and toppled him over a fraying sofa. "Here, what?" he repeated, getting unsteadily to his feet and dabbing at his nose with one finger. "Damme..."

"First blood," said the count. "I have tapped your claret." He was almost as self-satisfied at mastering phrases like this as he was at smashing his fist into this *scélérat*'s face. "I do not think you will send me a cartel, sir. I think you are a man who likes to see other men fight. But if you do send it, I will ignore it, because I am a brave man. In the meanwhile, I go and tell my principal that yours sends his apology. You can tell yours that mine withdraws his challenge. If you are not satisfied, I have more taps and you have more claret."

"Damme, you savage furriner—" said the other man.

Modrowski tapped more of his claret.

After this second blow, the man agreed to smooth matters with his principal. Modrowski drew on his gloves and left his victim drinking port to replace the tapped claret. The count slammed the door rather violently on his way out, to show his emotions toward this lily-livered fire-eater who called Poles and Hollanders 'frogs' and 'furriners.' This resulted in a short altercation with the landlady, who caught him downstairs to protest that he had near rattled the windows out of their frames, all but toppled her china off the shelves, and lud knew what else through all the house with his plaguey banging, and at the very least she'd want the carpenter sure, to mend the door, if not the glazier as well for half the windows. Since the landlady was a woman, this time the difference of opinion did not come to blows. After a soul-satisfying round or two of loud language on both sides, Modrowski gave her money for the door but damned his eyes if he would pay for any windows or china. Since the sum he flung down on the old deal-table in the lobby was more than generous for the door, the good woman was better content than she pretended, while Modrowski, by the time he had walked halfway down the first street, was whistling a mazurka from the Tatra Mountains.

True to his suspicion, no subsequent cartel arrived at his lodgings. Nor did either Hastings or his second make any move that would belie Modrowski's assurance to Conybeare that Hastings had indeed apologized (an assurance that Modrowski had no trouble reconciling with his own honor on grounds that, in relucting to fight, Hastings had tacitly signaled his apologies). So the storm blew over much as it had blown up, and the count resumed his preparations to septentrionate. He was particularly proud of having mastered this verb for making a journey northward.

54

Chapter 5.

Friday night (Saturday morning by now) was not rainy. There was that much to be thankful for. But it was cloudy, as if it might rain any moment. And even had it not been cloudy, Alice would still have waited in the gardenhouse that her uncle insisted upon calling a gazabo. She would have feared to pace the garden walks lest someone making nocturnal use of the chamber pot take a notion to peek through the shutters and espy her in the moonlight. (Was there a moon tonight at this hour? Alice realized with a shock that during the few months of her London sojourn, her country-bred awareness of the moon's phases, risings, and settings had slipped away like seldom-used Latin verbs.)

Even with the stars and moon (if there was one) hid by heavy, dark clouds, and Sir Toby's garden walls shutting out all but the faintest blush of the Mayfair street lamps, she cringed to remember how her half-boots had crunched on the gravel path from the door to the gardenhouse, and how she had walked into one of her grandfather's prized rosebushes—she hoped it had not been the Blushing Rhodanthe. Now and then, whenever her nerves became too tense for mere hand-wringing, she took a tiptoe turn up and down inside the gardenhouse, but she would not venture out upon the gravel again, nor attempt the lawn, not even with her boots removed and her umbrella to help ward off accidental stumblings into flowerbeds, bushes, or the pink and gray marble sundial and birdbaths.

The statuary, being made of white marble, was more visible. Unhappily so, for it looked rather like dim ghosts here and there about the garden and walls. Some of the pieces lacked heads and arms in imitation of genuine antiquities.

Her feet were cold and she thought she had pulled her right stocking on a splinter in the parquetted floor. At Viola's insistence, she had worn these old, sturdy leather half-boots for the first time in London, and they had made her feet sound like a cow's hoofs, so she had removed them for the time being. But she did not dare try to fetch her soft slippers out of her crammed portmanteau, lest she spill something in the darkness. Her hands were cold, too, despite her gloves. The rest of her was almost uncomfortably warm, so warm that she occasionally shivered in the practical muslin dress and the pelisse that was just a little heavy for London but might not be heavy enough for nights even farther north than her Lancashire home. But perhaps they would never get so far. And even if they did, they ought not need to be abroad at night any more after this. The rest of tonight and all day tomorrow, Viola planned, with a few false trails laid down behind them, should put them at a safe enough distance to spend every subsequent night at an inn. Alice hoped all these inns would be respectable. She supposed that all respectable inns must likewise be reasonably comfortable. She was going to be very, very tired by tomorrow night; she was glad that Vi intended to do all the driving.

She sat in her grandfather's wicker chair and pulled her feet up under her so as to try to warm them with her hands, a rather forlorn hope, and in this posture she dozed off, dreaming vaguely that she was a bird in a hailstorm. She might have lost her balance and toppled to the parquet if a horse's nicker in the lane behind the back garden wall had not woke her just in time.

The horse's hoofs had been the hailstones of her dream, and the beast sounded louder to her than the Manchester mills, which her father had once taken her to see. For a moment she thought of highwaymen, and one coming through the garden door she had left unlocked for Viola. Why had they not foreseen such a danger? She put on her boots and clutched her umbrella, prepared to scream and wondering if she could reach the garden door and bolt it before the highwayman came through.

Too late! The door creaked slowly outward—she heard more than saw it—and a single flash from a dark lantern zagged about and caught her eye through the ivied latticework of the gardenhouse wall. She blinked and backed away.

She heard something like a few whispered syllables, and then the figure shuttered its dark lantern and started stealthily down the path. By now Alice had remembered that highwaymen were not nearly so common nowadays as they had been in olden times, and that in any event they robbed travelers and left houses to horseless burglars; so she was almost sure the newcomer was only her friend Violet. How else would Vi have made her entrance, after all? But she was not quite sure enough to leave the gardenhouse and meet her. She hovered inside, peering out cautiously through lattice and window as the figure proceeded along the path to the middle of the garden.

Here it stopped, flashed another beam of lantern light around the place from wall to wall, then made for the gardenhouse.

Alice could endure the suspense no longer. Her right hand gripping the umbrella, she cupped her left to her mouth and whispered as loudly as she could, "Vi?"

The figure quickened its pace and gained the gardenhouse, stumbling a little as it tried to take the steps with its dark lantern closed. "Alice? Oh, good! I was afraid you weren't out yet, and I'd have to throw pebbles at your window, after all."

"Vi, oh, I'm so glad; for a minute I thought you were a burglar!"

"A burglar? Hmm." Viola struck a pose. "Do you know, that might have been an even better plan. If we were caught in the act of breaking into somebody's house—surely that would perturb them, if anything could!"

"And might make things very nasty for us!" said Alice, hoping that her friend was not actually contemplating such a change of plan. "I'll risk my poor reputation for this, Viola, but I shall *not* risk my neck."

"Oh, don't be silly, my guardian would set things right. We'd never see the inside of Newgate, let alone the dock. But we shouldn't have this chance for travel, neither," Viola added with a sigh. "No, our first plan is best. Hey! for the open road and the length of jolly England! Well, come on, we'd best be starting. Where's your things?"

"Here." Alice found her portmanteau and lifted it.

Viola came at once. "Allow me, madam, I am the gentleman. Oof! Hello," she went on, taking the portmanteau and setting it down again with a sharp thump. "Whatever have you packed, the fire irons?"

"Shhh! They'll hear you." Alice watched the house apprehensively, but no light appeared at any of the windows. "You told me to pack what I'd need for a fortnight, did you not? So I did. There's not a thing in my case but what I might very well need."

"Whew! Well, it's large enough to hold Crusoe's whole kit. We'll be in fine fettle if we should wash up on some desert island in the Avon or the Esk. We can use your portmanteau for our raft, too, if it floats."

"I think," said Alice, "that you are being very—very cavalier and sniggering. I have packed my bag, just as you told me, and I've waited out here in the cold for I don't know how long, and had nightmares, and—and might have been murdered by burglars before you came, and here I am ready to ruin my reputation and my whole life chasing off with you for this—this stupid wager, and I really think you could find better conversation than to make sport of my portmanteau. Here, I shall carry it myself. It's not too heavy for *me!*"

Viola sighed. "It must be the churning and spinning and all that you do in the country that makes your arms strong."

"I don't!"

"Then you might as well let me carry it, hadn't you? You can bring the lantern." Passing this piece of equipment to her friend, Viola once again seized the portmanteau and this time, prepared for its weight, handled it nicely.

They said nothing more as they proceeded from gardenhouse to gate, Viola leading with the portmanteau and Alice following with the lantern and her umbrella. The cabriolet waited unmolested in the lane, the horse chewing lazily at his reins where they were attached to the huge and rather superfluous iron door knocker in the shape of a griffon.

"Taffy!" Viola scolded, pushing his nose away from the reins. She then set to work coaxing her friend's portmanteau into place beside her own. "It'll only just fit. Any larger and we must have left it behind. We aren't riding by post chaise, you know."

"Yes, and how much room are your things taking?"

"A mere tiddle. My bag's no more than half the size of yours, and it holds Basty's brown coat and an extra pair of breeches, too. But then, I'm the gentleman," Viola added as she finished the task and moved to hand Alice up into the carriage. "If I were traveling in my own character, I imagine I'd want two portmanteaux each as large as yours, and we'd have to use the landau."

"Now you're patronizing me. I'd rather you teased." Alice jumped up unaided into the carriage. She found a bundle of dark cloth on the seat cushions and transferred it to her lap as she sat. Something small slipped from the bundle and fell to the carriage floor.

Viola picked up the dark lantern and stood playing with its slide until she seemed in danger of burning her fingers.

"What is this stuff?" Alice asked to break the silence, prodding the cloth bundle in her lap.

"Oh, that's your domino."

"My domino?"

"We'll be driving through the better parts of Town wherever possible, and don't know whom we may pass going home from balls and parties. So we'll wear dominoes and vizards, and everyone will think we've just been to a fancy dress ball, and won't worry about who we are and where we're going. They wouldn't know me, of course, though someone might mistake me for Sebastian and wonder when he'd come up to Town. But someone might recognize you."

"Oh. Then it must have been my vizard that fell to the floor just now."

Viola shone the dark lantern into the carriage at Alice's feet and together they searched the floor beneath the apron until they found the half-mask in a small coil of rope. Alice put it on and unfolded her domino.

"It's crimson," said Viola, "even though it looks black at night. Mine really is black.... But did you mean all that, Allie? About losing your reputation and ruining your life? If you'd really rather not, you needn't come. I'll find someone else. It'll be a bit harder to try Mrs. Beale without you, of course, but I daresay I can manage something, if I give my mind to it."

Alice thought of her friend attempting burglary, perhaps even trying to steal the Crown from the Tower. "Oh, no! I was only talking dramatically. You do it all the time, why shouldn't I?"

Viola's relief was audible. "That's all right, then."

Alice stood to put on her domino. Before she had it adjusted, Viola had gone round to the other side, taken her own vizard and domino from the driver's seat, and donned them.

"Hist!" said Viola. Alice turned her head to look, and sat down heavily on the cushions. Viola was shining the dark lantern's beam up at herself, and her broad smile stretched out beneath a fanciful half-face of something part satyr and part gargoyle.

"Vi!" said Alice. "And mine is just a simple silk thing with a tiny little frill."

"Oh, I didn't buy this especially. It's one Noddy used two or three Seasons ago. He gave it to Sebastian in hopes it might inspire him with a little mischief, but Basty just shunted it to the lumber room."

"Well, I think it very odd you should wear such a thing as that if you don't want people to recognize us. They're sure to remember it."

"Of course. If they see it tonight, they'll remember it for a week. And if anyone describes it to my guardian, Cousin Launcelot will be sure to remember who wore it first and give Noddy a rare shriving. Poor old Noddy, I do hope he'll find some good cock and bull to keep from letting the whole story slip out. But that's all a very long chance, and you're the one who must not be recognized tonight, in any event."

Viola untied Taffy, hopped up into the cabriolet, and took skillful hold of the reins. Alice pressed deeper into the cushions, wishing she had thought to take off her pelisse before putting on the domino, but at the same time enjoying the not entirely logical idea that each additional layer of clothing added to the likelihood no one would recognize her. Besides, she told herself, I've only made the most superficial acquaintance in London, except for Mrs. Beale and Vi and Grandfather and some of the Ayrsfords' circle. I don't have any serious beau or suitor, and it's not likely any London friends will ever come up to visit me in Lancashire, except Vi or Mrs. Beale—I hope. Vi is the one most likely to suffer from a lost reputation, she lives half her life in Town and knows almost everybody, so if she don't mind the risk, why should I? Maybe if they send her to the country for punishment, she can come and stop with me in Markham House....

They passed safely from London to the outlying villages. A couple of times in the less savory thoroughfares unkempt men seemed to eye them, filling Alice's head with new fear of footpads; but Viola brought out a large horse pistol, cocked it and rested it on one knee, and the derelicts kept their distance. Alice wondered if the mere sight of a gun would also scare away any highwaymen still loitering about outside the city, but the cabriolet traversed the fields from village to village without the travelers so much as hearing any hoofbeats other than Taffy's.

As the sun rose over a peaceful summer countryside some miles north of London, Alice relaxed at last, breathing out a long sigh, shedding her vizard, domino, and after a few moments her pelisse, and shaking out her golden curls. "Could you really have fired that pistol, Vi?"

"Of course, and so could you. All it needs to fire it is to pull the trigger. I can't answer for our aim, but at point-blank range I fancy we'd do well enough."

"And is it really charged?"

"What would be the use if it were not?" Viola had long ago removed her mask and shrugged off her domino. Now she laid the pistol, carefully uncocked, on the carriage floor.

"I don't think I'd know how to go about charging it," said Alice.

"I'll show you tonight. I used to watch my brother and my guardian and the gamekeepers do it whenever I had the chance, and I've refreshed my memory all week out of books from Basty's room and the library."

"I shouldn't have known the way out of London, either."

"No more should I this day last week, not nearly so well, anyhow. But I studied that, too, charted our course and memorized it like any pilot. And I think I did rather well, though I could have driven it faster if I'd had the chance of driving it by daylight once or twice beforehand."

"You did it wonderfully. Have you memorized all the rest of the way?"

"Very nearly. Of course I brought along *Kearsley's Guide* as well." Viola patted a bulge in her brother's coat pocket. "We may want to improvisate. You never know."

"What have you done to your hair?"

"Oh, just wet it and combed the curls out. They weren't natural, you know, like yours." Viola shook her straightened brown locks. "I wish it were long enough to draw back into an old-fashioned tail, but since it won't grow that much in a week, I may visit the first likely barber and have it trimmed a bit, if we have time."

Alice sighed again and settled back into the cushions. Taffy went at a gentle trot, the sunlight glistening on his hide to show he might as well have been named for his color as for his Welsh origin. Birds sang, leaves rustled, early workers were bringing their herd into a distant pasture, and although Middlesex was not Lancashire, the country maiden began to feel a little more comfortable.

Then the right wheel bounced on a rock and broke.

"Hold tight!" said Viola.

Alice had been holding tight from the instant the wheel touched the rock.

Taffy reared at the cracking sound and seemed for a moment about to bolt, but Viola kept control of the reins, steadying the horse with a firm yet flexible pressure and a monologue of soothing syllables, and soon brought them safely to a halt. Then she passed the reins to her friend and hopped down for a look at the wheel.

"Damnation!" she said. "I'd kick it, if I weren't afraid of shaking the carriage. There must have been a hidden flaw that nobody noticed."

"It felt like a very large rock," said Alice.

Viola glanced back. "So it was, if that's the one, and no doubt put there especially by wicked little plough-boys who think it great sport to watch gentlefolks' carriages break down or run out of control. But the blasted wheel still ought not to have broke, if it had been sound to begin with."

"Could the stone have been put there by highwaymen?" Alice asked, glancing round at the fields.

"Not likely. Not with so little cover. No, depend upon it they were ploughboys, probably hoping to prevent some gentleman from winning his race."

"Or perhaps it simply fell from a cartload."

"Well, I've a very good mind to leave it there," said Viola. "Filthy thing, it's spoiled my whole plan. I'd meant to leave the cabriolet on the Boroughbridge road a little beyond Hatfield."

"What shall we do now?"

Viola squared her shoulders and laughed. "Improvisate! I just said we might want to, though I didn't guess it would be so soon." She rubbed her chin, looking from Alice to Taffy to the cabriolet. "We will leave the rock where it is, and the carriage, too. We'll both mount Taffy and ride cross-country to the nearest village. I think it should be either Potter's Bar or Bell Bar if we strike out in that direction. Can you ride bareback?"

"I think so, if we don't gallop."

"I don't think we'll need to gallop. If things are going as they should at home, it'll be hours yet before we're missed. But we shouldn't lose too much time, either. And I think we must leave your portmanteau behind."

"Oh!" said Alice.

"Yes, I'm sorry, but I don't see how we can ask Taffy to carry us and all our luggage too. Even if it weren't so heavy, it'd still be deuced awkward. I'll have to leave my bag, too—oh, rot! They'll recognize it."

"They'll recognize the cabriolet, too," Alice pointed out. "And my portmanteau."

"Yes, but they're not supposed to know I've been with you from the start, only that I went out after you. And if they find Sebastian's things in my case...Why the devil didn't I think to pack everything in saddlebags!" Viola cried. "I say, it's really very easy to swear like a gentleman, ain't it? Well, we'll bundle up everything we can into our dominoes and tie 'em across Taffy's back, and I'll carry my case as far as I can and drop it somewhere in hopes they don't find it....No, I don't like to do that, either," she went on. "I've had this dear old portmanteau all my life, and I don't want to lose it forever, no matter how much Miss Merriweather and Noddy are staking on the outcome. Here, I'll empty everything out, go back, and drop it somewhere by the side of the road. With luck, our own people will be the ones to find it, so I'll get it back at last, and meanwhile it should give Cousin Launcelot something of a test to try his iron nerves. You can wrap up our things while I'm gone."

"Don't go very far."

"Oh, never fear, I'll be within calling distance, and I'll leave the gun with you, though I really don't think we've the least cause to worry. And do try to weed out a few of your things, Allie."

"What about the vizards?"

Viola thought a moment, grinned slowly, and shook her head. "No. I thought of putting 'em in my portmanteau for Cousin Launcelot to find, but that might tell him too much by half. We'll just leave 'em in the carriage."

Viola spread her black domino out on the road with a flourish as of a chambermaid casting the sheet out over the bed, and unceremoniously overturned the contents of her portmanteau upon its folds. Then she set off whistling in the direction they had come.

Alice sighed. "She might at least have handed me out of the carriage." But she got down and set to work. She sorted her own things, managing to leave about a fourth of them behind without too much pain, and rolling the rest neatly into her crimson domino. Not entirely in the sweetest temper, however, she treated Viola's things (or rather Sebastian's) almost as casually as Viola herself had done, flattening them a bit and rolling them up in the black domino pretty much as they had fallen, taking an unholy pleasure in the thought of what a mass of wrinkles her friend's next change of clothing would display.

Taffy stamped once or twice and nibbled at the roadside greenery. Alice made sure the ends of both rolls were well tucked in, arranged the articles she was leaving behind in her portmanteau, and was retying the straps when Viola strutted back to her.

"I found an excellent place for it," Viola announced. "Clean and leafy, with just one corner of leather showing. That will give them a puzzle how it came there. I hope it may suggest a scuffle. Of course, there's the chance some country people will find it instead, but they may be poor and reap some benefit from the prize."

"That's a very Christian thought," said Alice.

"It helps reconcile me to the risk of losing my case. A very tidy job, my love." Viola gave her rolled-up domino an unsuspecting pat.

Alice fashioned a halter for Taffy out of the rope her friend had thought to bring along in the carriage (and which had been entangling her toes much of the way from London), and Viola used a pocketknife of her brother's to cut up the reins for additional cording to fasten the improvised saddlebags. Within another hour, they were riding at a fast amble across the fields, aiming for the nearest church steeple. Both young ladies sat astride, Alice with her skirt hitched up to her knees. She hoped that no one would catch sight of them except at a distance.

Chapter 6.

It was nearly noon, and Noddy Duncton had been attempting for three quarters of an hour to prevent Lord Spottiswood from drubbing him too roundly at chess. Duncton disliked the game, but for that very reason it provided his most convenient means of keeping Spottiswood at hand to receive the full force of the first blow. His lordship had been upon the point of sallying forth for a botanical tour of the Chelsea Gardens when Duncton arrived, but the chance to torment his friend over his chessboard had proved a sufficient lure to hold him at home a while longer, and since Duncton found stamens and pollens even less exciting than rooks and pawns, the pretext was reasonably plausible.

There must have been a touch of the satanic in Lord Spottiswood's character, for even Noddy Duncton could see that his lordship was playing not so much chess as cat and mouse. Black could have trounced white in ten minutes, but instead sat content to pick at the pale army piecemeal, now and then throwing away a dusky pawn or bishop as if to tease by pretending encouragement. Duncton endured nobly in the cause, but breathed a secret sigh of relief when the housekeeper burst upon them at last.

"Mrs. Jones," said Lord Spottiswood.

In her twenty-some years with the family, Mrs. Jones had weathered out rats in the cellar, mice in the linen closet, a burglar in the drawing room, a Lothario in the garret bedrooms, two or three incipient fires in the kitchen, a bath that leaked over the new carpets, carriage accidents in the street below, and the bread riots of 1799, all with an aplomb approaching that of Lord Spottiswood's own. Now, however, her face was drawn, her bosom trembling, and her hand in a quiver as she held out to him a folded note.

He took it from her, unfolded it, skimmed the contents, and raised his left eyebrow. He then turned back to the chessboard and took his move by advancing his queen's rook to king four, putting white in checkmate before remarking, "My cousin and ward communicates that, learning a friend of hers was in the act of elopement yesterday evening, she has gone after the couple to offer her services as the young lady's companion. Had you any precognition of this, Duncton?"

"Spotty! What d'you take me for? Your game, by the way."

"I was aware of that." Spottiswood refolded the note and tapped it against his finger. "I felt it incumbent upon me to ask in light of the fact that for the best part of an hour you have sat meekly foundering through a game for which your sentiments approach abhorrence. A suspicious mind might have read your motive as anticipation of the crisis which appears to have befallen my house. Two further observations. First: That for a young person in the throes of an emotion so strong as to rouse her to this height of self-immolation, Viola writes in a remarkably steady hand." He passed the note to Duncton. "Second, twelve o'clock noon is an unusual time of day for her bedroom to be entered during the Season."

69

"She told Hertlow last night that's when she'd take her chocolate today," said Mrs. Jones.

"My point. As a rule, she either rings for her chocolate at a comparatively early hour, or desires not be wakened until one P.M. or later."

"Maybe she had some plans for today," said Duncton.

"That is possible. It is more possible, however, that she had already at the moment of setting the time for her morning chocolate formed her plans for last night, in which case I find it interesting that she should have arranged for us to discover her absence at noon." Spottiswood rose to his feet. "And I find it not far short of fascinating that her excess of magnanimity should not have extended to keeping secret the name of her ill-advised friend. Duncton, I believe that an immediate call upon Sir Toby Markham would not be out of reason. Mrs. Jones, I think I need not counsel you that the less said of this either above or belowstairs, the better."

She nodded. "Nobody knows so far but us and Hertlow, my lord, and I've told her to drink up Miss Ayrsford's chocolate herself and mind her tongue."

"I won't soon forgive m'self for making you miss your botanical tour, Spotty," said Duncton, who saw that his hopes were dashed for an early win of Miss Merriweather's money and that a longish chase actually did loom ahead.

If discretion had been the keynote at Ayrsford House, it had not in Sir Toby's domicile. Calcutta House was in turmoil, its servants rushing about like started grouse. It was a kitchenmaid who opened the door to Lord Spottiswood and Mr. Duncton, admitted them to the lobby, took their cards in her hand and went in search of her master, "like a Christian martyr in search of the lion," as Mr. Duncton remarked.

Lord Spottiswood hung up his hat. "Markham may

remain unaware that my ward is involved in this affair. In his unenlightenment, he will be no more anxious to receive us than to receive any unconcerned third party. We may need to force our way in." He produced his pocketwatch and compared it with the tall clock in the lobby. "We will allow them ten minutes to make their move regarding our presence."

They waited eight minutes and thirty seconds by both timepieces. The largely unseen tumult in the house behind them was punctuated with an occasional roar from the old city knight. At length the maid returned, taking conscientiously deep breaths, and led the gentlemen into the breakfast room, where they found Mrs. Beale and Miss Merriweather partaking of a light nuncheon. Despite the confusion around her and the teasing of her companion, the widow remained an island of calm in an ocean of turbulence. Duncton breathed more easily and eyed the two places set but not occupied beside the ladies.

"Your lordship," said Mrs. Beale. "Mr. Duncton. Will you join us? I cannot linger over luncheon, but such time as I can spare is at your disposal."

"We will join you gladly, madam. Reason dictates that the body should be fortified against a strenuous undertaking." Spottiswood handed Viola's note to Mrs. Beale.

She read it and raised her left brow. "So it appears you will join us for more than luncheon. You may as well take the unused covers," she went on. "They were laid for Miss Markham and Sir Toby. You already know why hers is not needed today, and if he were persuaded to eat in his present state, it might lead to sickness and delay in the carriage."

"So she's ordered 'em to pack up a picnic for him instead," said Miss Merriweather.

The corners of Mrs. Beale's mouth twitched slightly

upward. "You don't ask why Lord Spottiswood spoke of a strenuous undertaking, ma'am, or I of his joining us for more than luncheon. Your lordship?" She directed a glance at him.

He understood it at once. "Miss Merriweather certainly has an excellent right, being the young lady's duenna."

Mrs. Beale passed Viola's note to Miss Merriweather, who looked at it and jumped to her feet, crying, "Ye cats and little goldfishes!"

"Possibly an applicable sentiment," remarked Spottiswood, "but one which I do not recollect your having used before now."

"Oh, my poor, dear chick! What's to become on 'em? Well, Launcelot," said the old lady, "you needn't think to chase off after 'em without me."

"Our party has certainly increased within moments," said Mrs. Beale. "But I trust this new complexion of things won't prevent you from finishing your meal. I, for one, shall rest a little easier in the hope that your charge and mine may really be together."

"Aye, I daresay 't is true enough that misery loves company," returned Miss Merriweather.

Lord Spottiswood helped himself to three boiled eggs and two slices of bread and butter. "How and when do you plan to leave, Mrs. Beale?"

"Within the hour. We had meant to take the phaeton for greatest speed, drive straight up by the shortest route and, if we fail to overtake them due to their having chose a different road, to await them at the Border."

"And if they find the young 'uns waiting for them instead, and already yoked together by yon blacksmith," said Miss Merriweather in tones of mimicry, "then they'll have to hope for the best in this Romeo as has turned the poor girl's head. But I say he's naught but one o' these rascally fortune hunters, most like, and a rare time you'll catch of it from Captain Markham when he comes home again."

Mrs. Beale sipped her sherry. "Perhaps Viola may talk that prudence into Alice's head which I was mistaken in believing already there. Or perhaps Viola, being a notable romantic, may win this mysterious beau away from Alice and marry him herself," she added with a look at the older woman.

"Better they should ruin their reputations," snapped the spinster, "than saddle 'emselves with a bad husband."

Mrs. Beale heard even this social heresy without blinking. "I agree, ma'am. But if the young ladies are indeed together with the unknown gentleman, it is just possible that both their reputations may yet be saved with only minor injury, despite their youth."

Lord Spottiswood took a slice of cake. "I conceive that Viola would delight in a ruined reputation, at least for a Season or two. After that, we might have to match her with Duncton for want of a more respectable offer."

"Here!" exclaimed Duncton.

Miss Merriweather cackled. "Aye, that might do well enough for Mistress Vi. As for little Mistress Markham, we might let her marry her fortune hunter and then have you call him out and save her from wedded misery, Launcelot."

Spottiswood broke off a bite of bread. "Sir Toby or Captain Markham would be the more logical man to perform that service for Miss Markham, madam. Nor would I much incline to perform it immediately for my own ward."

"You would put her through a hard school, sir," said Mrs. Beale, "in requiring her to live long enough with a rogue to appreciate the advantages of widowhood."

"We do not yet know he is a rogue," Spottiswood pointed out. "The circumstance of an elopement to Scotland is not promising, but young men as well as young women are sometimes prone to romantic flights."

"Exactly." Mrs. Beale cut a slice of cake. "And with her father at sea and her grandfather prejudiced against any potential aspirant younger than sixty or lower placed in life than an earl, one understands how they might conceive the need for desperate measures. One has more difficulty understanding how they found opportunity for plotting."

"Further speculation must prove fruitless until we have more evidence," said Spottiswood.

"All the more reason to avoid delay. Madam," Mrs. Beale went on, turning to Miss Merriweather, "if you mean to accompany us, you might prefer choosing what you need for the journey from my things, rather than wait until yours can be sent round for. Hennings can pack them up for you. Gentlemen, perhaps essentials can be found for you from Sir Toby's wardrobe, or Captain Markham's old things. It won't be elegant, but speed may be the greater consideration."

"I not only agree, madam," said his lordship, "I depute Mr. Duncton to choose my spare linens while you and I discuss our itinerary arrangements."

"Well!" Miss Merriweather stood up. "Old birds pack light, and I see I'd best leave the young appetites to batten proper. Come on, Noddy, and we'll see our needs all packed up before theirs are, yet."

Duncton made a mild protest. "My own appetite is not precisely aged, ma'am."

Miss Merriweather slapped a piece of cold tongue between two muffins and put it into his hand. "Here. If 't was good enough for Lord Sandwich, 'tis too good for you."

Duncton looked at Spottiswood and Mrs. Beale, hastily swallowed half a glass of Madeira, and followed Miss

Merriweather from the room. In the passage, they held a muttered consultation on the state of their wager.

"We might as well leave 'em for ten minutes," she began in tones of disgust. "It's a corker if they ain't cracked yet, they'll keep cool as watercress until we're on the road at least."

"I take it that was a fair sample of how she received the initial shock."

"Aye. But likewise how my Launcelot stood up to the blow, I'll wager."

"First round even," he concurred. "But the Beale had both you and Sir Toby setting up a buzz about her. Wouldn't care to stake another thousand, would you?"

"Done, you young looby, and I'll give you two to one, what's more."

"Not necessary, ma'am. In fact, I was about to offer you those same odds."

"Huh! Well, call it even, then," said the old lady, as if conferring a favor. They shook hands and proceeded upstairs to find servants and ransack their hosts' dressing rooms.

Meanwhile, Lord Spottiswood and Mrs. Beale looked at one another across the luncheon board.

"That pair knows something," he remarked.

"I was much inclined to suspect it."

"I should not be greatly surprised if there proved to be no mysterious seducer in the case and our two maidens were to be found hiding with female friends here in Town."

"Indeed, I rather fancy that to be the situation, though of course there will probably be a father, a brother or two, and possibly a grandfather or an uncle in the house as well as the female members of the friendly family. Have you tried the jellied asparagus?"

He had not, the side dish being beyond his reach,

but served himself eagerly when, in the absence of any servant to bring the delicacy to his side of the table, the hostess passed it to him. "Having formed this opinion," he resumed, "you naturally suggested to Markham your search might begin in the houses of your closer acquaintance?"

"I have drawn up a mental list of the likeliest addresses. You will supplement it, of course. Viola's acquaintance in and about London must be larger than Alice's, and I think it probable that Viola was the guide in this prank."

"I think it highly probable. If you have the opportunity, you may pass on to Markham's cook my compliments upon the asparagus."

"I thought you would appreciate it, with your taste for vegetables. Unfortunately, Sir Toby could not endure the strain of stopping to search London and its environs whilst under the impression that every hour brings his grandchild closer to Gretna Green. I would let him chase northward and stay to search the city myself, but I have some fears for him if he is allowed to drive off unattended except by a few of his servants."

"Whom he employed more for their appearance than their sense."

"Precisely. Your lordship is perceptive."

"It is an avocation of mine. The human condition in general makes a rather diverting spectacle, especially among the pampered classes who have little need to worry their heads with the essential needs of daily life."

Mrs. Beale nodded and chose a pear from the fruit tray. "That is the reason you find us about to embark upon what may well prove a chase for wild geese before we can approach the work of scouring the city."

He cored and sliced but did not peel an apple. "Speed remains a prime consideration. Duncton and I can flank the carriage in place of outriders, but as I recall Markham's phaeton, Cousin Merriweather as a third will make the fit uncomfortable. Might Markham also ride horseback?"

"That could have unfortunate results. He was not the most notable equestrian in youth, being too much the man of business, and at this period of his life I would sooner trust your Cousin Merriweather on a galloping mount. Would you trust her to drive?"

The corners of his mouth quirked slightly. "I would trust her to challenge Noakes or Bampton to race a team to Tonbridge Wells, and I should probably back her to win. But I would hesitate to put the reins into her hands when the safety of other riders in the same carriage would be in question."

"I was a tolerable horsewoman in youth," said Mrs. Beale as if her youth were long past, "and believe I could quickly accustom myself to the saddle again."

"When this business is over, madam, perhaps you would join me for an occasional ride round the park."

Mrs. Beale did not consider a polite smile incompatible with her dignity. This, however, was the extent of her reply to Lord Spottiswood's not completely relevant proposal. "The difficulty," she went on when the smile had been folded and put away again, "is that since you would not trust Miss Merriweather and I would not trust Sir Toby with the reins, I will be needed to drive, unless we were to expand the party by including a coachman and other servants, which I think would prove unwieldy and unwise. Though we must abandon the phaeton, my landaulet may be made to hold three with comfort, and I think we will not sacrifice too much speed."

"It would be logical," he said with a lack of emotion that might have cost even him extra care in making the speech, "to suggest that we split our party. Either Duncton or I could handle the reins of the phaeton, while you and Miss Merriweather began searching the city."

"That would be a very logical suggestion," she agreed.

"Can you defeat it with a counterproposal of equal logic, madam?" To say there was a note of hope in his lordship's voice might have been to judge him by one's own sentiments.

"I cannot answer for the logic of the counterargument," she replied, "but we may discover a key to our young ladies' behavior by close observation of how Miss Merriweather and Mr. Duncton comport themselves, and they both seemed bent upon the adventure."

"Very true," said Lord Spottiswood. "And not totally illogical."

Mrs. Beale rang for a servant and directed him to have the landaulet rather than the phaeton readied for the journey.

Chapter 7.

They found the broken cabriolet between Hadley-Pillar and Hatfield.

"It is, of course, my ward's carriage," said Lord Spottiswood, "and I trust Viola will have sufficient monies of her own remaining at the end of her adventure to pay for its repair, that being the compact made between us when I presented it to her on the occasion of her eighteenth birthday. Madam, this appears to give the lie to our theory that they are hiding with friends in London."

"Unless they had it in mind from the beginning to circle back," said Mrs. Beale.

"The accident, at least, was genuine," said his lordship.

Sir Toby went into what in a female would have been called vapors and had to be revived with Miss Merriweather's smelling bottle. Lord Spottiswood and Mrs. Beale descended for a more thorough examination of the cabriolet, and Noddy Duncton turned his mount to retrace the path of the accident as well as he could on the dry road. Mrs. Beale found the vizards beside the dark lantern on the carriage floor. She quietly pointed them out to his lordship. He picked up the more extravagant mask, nodded, said, "Duncton's," picked up the other as well and tucked them both beneath his coat and vest. When more or less recovered, Sir Toby jumped down from the landaulet and searched the broken carriage and all the road around for blood, though both Spottiswood and Mrs. Beale assured him there was none.

"Miss Ayrsford's carriage, eh?" the city knight was reasoning out. "And Miss Ayrsford went after 'em, she didn't go with 'em. Then Alice warn't in the accident, eh? Then my little Alice'll be safe and sound?"

"We have no evidence to suppose she is other than safe and sound, Sir Toby," said Mrs. Beale. "She does, however, seem to have been in the carriage at the time of the accident."

The widow showed Sir Toby his granddaughter's portmanteau, with some of her things still within, and he succumbed once more to his emotions. Miss Merriweather t'sked and descended to take his head into her lap as he lay stretched on the road and hold her bottle to his nose again.

Duncton came galloping back to his companions and pulled his horse to a stop on seeing this tableau. "Excellent thing in its way that we left all our servants at home," he remarked. "Know enough about our little foibles as it is, they do."

"I congratulate you, ma'am," said Mrs. Beale to Miss Merriweather. "I should have thought to bring hartshorn. Rarely using it myself—"

"Aye, we know you never need anything of its kind," said Miss Merriweather, "but you ought to ha' known Sir Toby, ma'am, stopping in his house all this blessed Season."

"I ought to have known," the widow agreed, "but we were agitated this morning. What are you bringing us, Mr. Duncton?"

Duncton held it up and tossed it to Lord Spottiswood, who caught it neatly and observed, "Viola's case. I suspected she was not so much agitated as to have rushed away to the Scottish border with no traveling necessaries."

"It must be very light now," said Mrs. Beale, "judging from the way Mr. Duncton threw and your lordship caught it."

"It is empty," Spottiswood replied.

"Robbed!" Sir Toby sat up and demonstrated the restoration of his wits by shouting. "They've been set on, robbed, and murdered!"

"Twaddle!" snapped his nurse, her own impatience getting the better of her. "There ain't any blood. Most hightobymen as murders folk leaves 'em bloody by the carriage. More likely kidnapped and took to ransom," she added with a look at Mrs. Beale. "Let's hope as they want a good ransom price more than they want a bit o' female comfort."

"We shall send letters home from the next village or posting house," said Mrs. Beale, "directing that any ransom demands delivered to either of our houses be paid at once. Lord Spottiswood, do you think it probable such demands may be delivered?"

"I think it highly improbable," he replied. "Highwaymen intent on robbery and ransom would have taken the portmanteaux with all their contents."

"They've took the horse, ain't they?" said Sir Toby.

"Precisely, sir," said Spottiswood.

"But with no sign of a struggle," said Mrs. Beale.

"Have you noticed, madam, how neatly the reins have been cut?" his lordship inquired of the widow.

"Very likely in order to tie up those necessaries they carried with them," she responded.

"My own thought exactly."

"But look here, Spotty," Duncton interjected, "what

do you make of Vi's kit having been tossed into the bushes half a mile back?"

"Without further information, I make nothing definite of it. I assume that my romantic young ward will provide the further information when we find her."

"Robbed and kidnapped and—and belike murdered," cried Sir Toby, "and there you stand talking like it was the latest news from India!"

"In fact, Sir Toby," said Duncton, "I think you take the latest news from India more passionately than our gracious Mrs. Beale takes the young ladies' disappearance, eh?"

"Have you observed, madam," Lord Spottiswood asked Mrs. Beale, "that the drama suggested from the evidence before us leaves little place for the mysterious bridegroom?"

"Unless he rode his own mount alongside the cabriolet," she said. "The road is too dry for any clear impressions."

Sir Toby boiled over. "But what's t' be done? Damme, what's to be done?"

"Presumably," said Lord Spottiswood, "they have taken what they could, mounted the carriage horse, and pursued their way. They may have struck out upon any bypath or even across country, but I believe our own best course will be keeping to the main road, either on to Scotland or back to London."

"Damme, we should call out the runners!" said Sir Toby.

"Do you prefer to return to London, sir?" inquired Mrs. Beale.

"Gadsookers, no!" said Miss Merriweather. "We can drop 'em a line from yonder village at the same time we post our letters home about the ransom."

"In my opinion, the runners would lose their time," said Lord Spottiswood. "You will have observed that upon the wheel being rendered useless, the carriage was brought to such a stop as demonstrates a capable and collected driver holding the reins. Some of the praise must also fall to the horse. By the report of our senior stableman, the horse will have been Taffy, a sturdy, gentle beast highly unlikely to attempt shaking off his riders. Between my ward and her favorite pony, I do not apprehend any serious harm will come to a pair of young ladies in the English countryside by daylight, and we may hope they have sufficient sense to stop at a respectable house well before nightfall."

"I believe, sir," said Mrs. Beale, "that some share of the praise may also be owing to my charge, who must have helped bring the accident to a bloodless conclusion by keeping her seat calmly and quietly. Despite her uncharacteristic role in this elopement, I still credit Alice with enough prudence to temper Viola's wilder excesses."

His lordship lifted one eyebrow and slipped the two vizards to Mrs. Beale under cover of the open traveling case. "It is your charge, madam, who packed the larger portmanteau."

"In a young person of her inexperience, packing too much for a journey is a further sign of prudence." Depositing the vizards beneath a lace fichu, Mrs. Beale held up a soft bedroom slipper and a jar of cosmetic cream. "Even without knowing precisely what she carried with her, I should guess she made a wise choice in what she left behind when circumstances dictated a smaller load."

"What, ma'am, you didn't go through her dressing room and list up everything she took away with her?" said Miss Merriweather.

Mrs. Beale probably caught the sarcasm, but did not acknowledge it. "The fact of her absence being plain, listing her possessions would hardly have warranted the time. Moreover, it would have been very difficult, since I do not have a list of all Alice's possessions in Calcutta House, to tell me what was missing and what was not. Have you a list of Viola's things, Miss Merriweather?"

"Of course she don't," Duncton put in. "What about all their stuff here?"

"We shall carry their portmanteaux along." Mrs. Beale replaced the slipper and cosmetic cream and closed the case. "There is room in the boot of my carriage, and the young ladies may welcome the convenience when we find them."

"You'll spoil 'em, ma'am," said Miss Merriweather. "Best throw their cases in the ditch by way of honest chastisement."

"And waste some tolerably useful portable property?" Mrs. Beale fastened the portmanteau straps. "We should have wit to devise a thriftier punishment."

"I trust we'll find a competent wheelwright in Hatfield," said Lord Spottiswood. "One who may be entrusted to take care of the cabriolet for a sum down and the rest to be paid on our return."

"That little parcel of a cousin of yours can turn you right round her finger, Spotty," said Duncton. "Easy enough t' see how she expects you'll forgive her this caper in half a minute. Why not leave her cab out here till we bring her back, and give her a lesson?"

"I might have been so tempted," said his lordship, "but for the example Mrs. Beale sets us in the careful husbanding of this world's goods. You need have no fear but that the bill for all necessary repairs will be tendered to my ward in due course. So have a care, Duncton, or in the end she may obtain the money from you."

"Hang 'em all, I'll pay all the expenses!" said Sir Toby. "Just bring me my girl safe and sound and let me thrash the villain to an inch of his life who's tried t' steal her away!"

Sir Toby was perhaps the only member of the party who still had any great confidence in the existence of the fortune-hunting bridegroom.

Whilst Lord Spottiswood searched out a good wheelwright in Hatfield and Mrs. Beale sat in a private parlor of the Salisbury Arms, giving Sir Toby words of encouragement and writing the letters for him and Lord Spottiswood to sign and post home, Duncton and Miss Merriweather conferred over tankards of ale in the common room.

"Well," she demanded, "and what about the hartshorn, eh? Didn't she as good as confess she was too flustered this morning to think o' bringing it along?"

"I suppose she might have done, ma'am, if you hadn't cut in on her. But though the confession might have been there, the manner robbed it of any meaning. But what about the way Spotty tried to argue which of 'em has the cooler head, Vi or Alice?"

"Argue? You call that argufying, pup? Beshrew me, 't was naught but a bit o' mild baiting, and not much of that, neither."

"Baiting? Or flirting, perhaps?"

"Well, it warn't flustering, my boy. 'T was no more than Launcelot's little humor, and if you don't allow Beale's hartshorn, I don't allow Launcelot's humor."

"Still neck and neck, then." Duncton sighed and called for more ale. "It promises to be a long and dusty road that lies ahead of us, ma'am."

Chapter 8.

Riding Taffy and asking directions of the country folk (somewhat to Alice's embarrassment), the two young adventuresses had reached Mims, where they were able to hire a tim-whiskey and drive on after a short rest and a meal to St. Albans. Here they had the fortune to meet a northbound mail coach with only one passenger. Viola quickly arranged for Taffy's comfortable accommodation in the stables of the Woolpack Inn while Alice bought all three remaining places in the mail coach, one apiece for herself, her 'brother,' and their bundled possessions. When another traveler joined them at Woburn, they took their bundles into their laps.

The other passengers were personable gentlemen, no doubt good fellows amongst their own acquaintance but no more than bland and untroublesome company to the strangers. They could not help a few curious glances at the original use of dominoes for portmanteaux, but they accepted Viola's explanation that it enabled one to carry one's things along even in the mail coach, and they did not appear to question the sex of Mr. Caesar Williams (Alice had persuaded Viola against using the full name 'Cesario' adopted by Viola's literary namesake in Shakespeare's play) or his brotherly relationship to the supposed Miss Williams.

The mail coach arriving in Leicester that evening, Mr. and Miss Williams put up in adjoining bedrooms at the White Horse. Alice pointed out that it would be thriftier to take a single room, but Viola replied it would also be much less prudent, even for supposed brother and sister; and besides, both Miss Merriweather and dear old Noddy Duncton had been so generous that the young ladies might never need to use any of Viola's own blunt all the way to Scotland. They treated themselves to sleeping until eight the following morning, which was adventurously early for Viola to wake and only a little later than Alice was used to rising on summer mornings in the country. They examined the inn's horse trough, which their host reaffirmed had been made from the coffin of Richard the Third, and pronounced it interesting. Mr. Williams found a barber to trim his hair, explaining that its crudely kempt state was due to a long walking tour, only just completed, through the wild regions of Wales. Miss Williams bought three pairs of the locally manufactured stockings and Mr. Williams visited a single curiosity shop, purchased one of the locally unearthed Roman coins, and made a solemn vow to return some day and examine all the traces of romantic history hereabouts with the closeness they deserved. Mr. Williams also purchased proper saddlebags and hired horses for himself and his sister.

They rode without incident as far as Derby, Alice on the kind of sidesaddle to which she was accustomed and Viola hugely enjoying the feel of both feet in stirrups. At Derby, having had enough exercise for the day, they took places in a post chaise leaving from the King's Head and carrying them to the Staffordshire town of Leek.

By coincidence, the chaise drew into the courtyard of the Swan with Two Necks from the south at about the same time a lone equestrian arrived from the north. The cut of his clothing very much resembled that preferred by Alice's father, so that she might have supposed him an officer of some merchantman, but his bearing on horseback and the ease with which he swung down from the saddle belied any thought of his being more used to the ocean than the land. His horsemanship impressed the young ladies all the more when they noticed that his right sleeve was pinned up to the breast of his coat.

"Oh, Vi!" Alice murmured in her companion's ear. "The brave gentleman! And he is so very handsome, too!"

"Caesar, if you please," Viola whispered back. "Shall we sup with him tonight?"

"But we are perfect strangers..."

"Tush, my dear, that's a mere trifle when you are traveling with your brother."

Miss Williams hung back, but Mr. Williams swaggered across the yard to where the one-armed stranger was entrusting his mount to a gaping stableboy. Perhaps it was due to her assumed identity as another male, but Caesar Williams did not find the horseman so overpoweringly handsome. Blond, of course, and blue-eyed, with long, lean cheeks and a becomingly sun-bronzed skin. Broad shoulders, too—the arm must be truncated near the elbow—and a most gentlemanly way of turning his legs, suggestive of elegance on the dancing floor. All in all, had Viola been in her own character she would not have minded standing up with him for a set, but he was too thin and wore too earnest a countenance to flutter her pulse. Though of course his missing arm might account for his serious expression.

"A fine piece of horseflesh, sir," said Mr. Williams, rejoicing in the freedom granted by a pair of breeches.

"Tolerable, sir, tolerable." The stranger smiled, and Mr. Williams noted crinkles at the corners of his eyes and thought they augured well. Were his cheeks a little fuller, the right one might dimple. "This Brown Jack was the best Macclesfield had for hire," he went on, "but I won't say I've never rode a better."

"I regret to hear it. Your report of the Macclesfield cattle, I mean. My sister and I had hoped to spend part of our own journey tomorrow in the saddle, but if you have taken the last decent mount between here and Stockport or Manchester..."

Again the stranger smiled. "Well, sir, if there are three tolerable mounts to be found here in Leek tomorrow morning, I'll leave two of 'em for you and your sister. That's the lady over there?"

"Yes. Miss Williams, and I am Mr. Williams. Your very obedient, sir." Mr. Williams extended his right hand, drew it back, and quickly substituted his left.

"Standeven. James Standeven, Lieutenant, Royal Horse Guards. Soon to be late of the Royal Horse Guards. At your service, Mr. Williams." Mr. Standeven shook his new acquaintance's hand. Viola observed with growing pleasure that Standeven had accepted Mr. Williams as an adult. She had not feared he would see through her masculine disguise. No one else seemed to have so far, her voice being naturally low and her stride perfected before she left home. But she had rather feared he might patronize her as a schoolboy, her chin being so obviously unused to the razor.

"Mr. Standeven, sir," she went on, "my sister and I were hoping for the pleasure of your company at such a supper as the Double-Necked Swan may provide."

There passed over his face an expression that she was later to describe as anticipated long-suffering. He patted his empty sleeve. "To hear the tale of how I lost this?"

"Not unless you wish to tell it," she said hastily. "Believe me, sir, our only motive was the desire for congenial company tonight. Our fellow traveler from Derby was not congenial, being a damned commercial with nothing in his brain except cheap chinaware. He descended at Ashborn to be replaced by a person with a jolly red nose, whose conversation was mostly snores and who rolled—almost literally, I assure you—from the chaise at Winkhill. We've been alone ever since." She shrugged. "Sisters and brothers tend to be at loggerheads in the best of times, sir, as you'll know if you've one or two of your own, and the end of a long day's travel in warmish weather hardly classes as the best of times."

"So you're willing to take a chance on the first stranger to save you from your own conversation, eh?" Mr. Standeven's cheek gave further indication of its desire to dimple. "Well, Mr. Williams, I never had a sister. I've often envied the men so blessed. But I do have a brace of brothers."

"Ah! Then you take my meaning."

"I think so, and if I'm to rescue the lady from another quarrel with her loving brother over the mutton tonight, maybe you'd better introduce us straightway."

Deciding that he did not lack totally in humor and that she approved of him, Viola led him back to Alice. "My dear, allow me to present Mr. Standeven, soon to be late of the Royal Horse Guards." This much information, she judged, must be unobjectionable, since he had provided it himself. "Mr. Standeven, my sister, Miss Williams."

"Mr. Standeven." Like Viola, Alice mechanically extended her right hand. He took it at once, before she could rectify the oversight, and instead of attempting to shake it left-handed, bowed and raised it to his lips, causing her to blush.

"Good news, sister," said Viola. "Mr. Standeven has agreed to sup with us. If you'll excuse me, sir, I'll just go in and arrange for a private parlor, if such a thing is to be had."

Mr. Standeven let go of Alice's fingers. "I can be with you in half an hour. Let me see to my horse. He might have to carry me again tomorrow, you know. And I think I can find a clean stock in my kit. If half an hour's convenient for you, ma'am?"

"Oh, very convenient," said Alice. "Quite convenient, sir."

"*Au 'voir*, then, ma'am."

"*A bientôt*, sir."

Mr. Standeven made another bow and returned to the stableboy who held his horse.

"Well," Viola teased when he was out of earshot, "and what do you suppose that pretty lapse into French meant on both your parts?"

"Nothing at all." Alice's blush had not faded. "What should it mean?"

"To a disinterested bystander, it might seem you were both desperate to cloak the state of your nerves."

"Why, we only just met, and we're to see him for one evening and then he'll be gone again, probably forever. It was nothing but...but polite gallantry."

"My dear," said Viola, "I have studied polite gallantry, and that was more than polite gallantry. It was a moment of sincere bashfulness."

"Oh. Well, if we're to bespeak a private parlor, we'd best go and do it."

"One thing," Viola added. "He seems excessively shy about his arm. I think perhaps it's a recent loss. We had better not question him about it."

"Of course not." Alice looked almost as if she had

been insulted. "I never intended to do so. In fact, to be safe, I think we had better not ask him anything about his personal history at all."

"Well, agreed," said Viola a little reluctantly. "Unless he brings it up himself, of course." She had hoped that with tact it would still be possible to draw out tales of war and adventure in foreign climes. But likely, she comforted herself, being a gentleman, I shall have him alone for an hour over port.

They went in, bespoke their accommodations, and repaired to their bedrooms to freshen their toilettes.

Last night in Leicester, finding her spare garments wrinkled to distraction by her friend's method of packing, Viola had simply had them ironed at the White Horse and then packed them herself with much greater care in the new saddlebags. She had worn the brown coat for travel today, and was now pleased to find the green one in smooth enough condition to be worn at once. She changed her shirt, put on the tan breeches and striped vest to go with the green coat, tied a fresh saffron-colored neckcloth in a simple fall, and went to see how Alice was getting on.

"I do wish," said Viola on entering her friend's room, "that you had brought something with a lower neck."

"I don't even own anything with a lower neck." Alice adjusted her cashmere shawl over a jaconet muslin bodice that really needed no aid to modesty.

"You do. Your pink silk goes a good half inch lower. And this one ain't even a party gown. It's an afternoon frock."

"I thought it would be more practical. I had brought my pale green, you know, but you made me leave whatever I could behind when the carriage wheel broke. And you did read me a lecture on the virtues of traveling unburdened, did you not?"

"Well, the light green all but goes up into collar

points, but it would have gone better with my coat. We'd have looked like brother and sister indeed!"

"It wouldn't. I saw them together when I was rolling up our things yesterday. They were not at all harmonious shades. Besides, if I were to come at him like a flirt, with my bosom showing down to...down to here, you know...I might really make him bashful."

"Or draw him out. You don't know much about gentlemen, Allie."

"And you, I suppose, are as wise as anyone. Well, I've had Mrs. Beale to talk with, and she's a widow. Your Miss Merriweather never was married."

"Ah, but she was a great coquette in her day. I shouldn't be surprised if she enjoyed a few of the advantages of marriage without any of its drawbacks." Viola winked.

"Shame!" said Alice, and changed the subject without further ado. "I wonder if it was only that I was the first woman he had spoke with since losing his arm that made him a little bashful?"

"Not the first woman, I shouldn't think. Not even if he just lost it aboard the ship home and has come straight inland. There's too many towns between here and the nearest port, not to mention the nearest port itself. But I shouldn't be at all surprised if you was the first respectable lady he's been introduced to since the accident, or whatever it was."

"Well, I shall bear that in mind—all of it—and behave myself accordingly."

"Don't be a clotpoll, Allie. All gentlemen do it. Dash my points if I ain't half tempted to try for an amorous adventure myself this trip." Viola hitched her thumbs beneath her lapels.

"Viola!"

"Well, isn't it vastly unfair that the men can misbehave that way and we can't? Oh, don't worry, my dear, it would be a very rare gentleman indeed before I would trust him with my secret, and I doubt we won't have time to find such a creature even if one exists between here and Scotland. And I won't try to push you into a flirtation with Mr. Standeven. But if you try to be a Puritan about such things and wait for an untouched bridegroom, then I think you'd best study Miss Merriweather's style of living, for you'll probably die a spinster, and I'm afraid you won't have so much fun about it as she does."

"You needn't give me another homily, Vi. You've done quite enough to spoil my chances for a respectable husband as it is."

Again Viola felt that little twinge of guilt. *Alice is so very straitlaced!* she thought. *Perhaps I ought not have brought her into the adventure.* "Why do you think I'm matchmaking so desperately for you now?" she said as lightly as she could.

"No...no, I didn't mean that, Vi. Not as it sounded."

"Don't worry. We're simply squabbling like true brother and sister. No one would ever take us for lovers running away to Gretna. Oh, and I've thought of something else. We'll let 'Vi' stand for 'Victor.' Caesar was famous for his victories, so it'll be a logical nickname, and we won't have to worry about your sometimes forgetting and calling me Vi in public."

"That will be very nice. Especially as we hadn't a good nickname for 'Caesar' before."

Mr. Williams held out his elbow. "And so, my dearest sister, had we not better be joining our new acquaintance?"

Chapter 9.

They found Mr. Standeven waiting for them. His coat and trousers had been brushed and his boots polished. Light as he seemed to be traveling, he had put on a fresh shirt with ruffles at the wrist and a flowered waistcoat as well as a clean neckcloth. The neckcloth was wound several times around and then folded over and fastened with a small gold stockbuckle. The effect was neat, and Viola mused that the loss of one arm might actually have shortened the time Mr. Standeven required to dress by forcing him to find so simple an expedient for a process widely reported to cost gentlemen of fashion a dozen attempts with as many neckcloths whenever they decorated their throats. (Not that she had ever witnessed the painstaking performance. In matters of dress, her brother Sebastian was a Quaker, her friend Noddy Duncton a careless Guy, and her cousin Launcelot a Utilitarian, so that she considered herself very clever to do as well as she did with her own stock.)

Mr. Standeven noticed her eyes lingering on his neckcloth and put his hand up to touch the stockbuckle. "Yes, it is awkward. I'll need to rely on a valet when I get to London."

"Oh, I ain't half sure of that," said Viola. "I've got a kinsman achieved quite a resounding success this Season with a black silk handkerchief." She proceeded to recount the famous episode of the game of brag, and between this, a reasonably good bottle of sherry, and general compliments on each other's appearance, the awkwardness was smoothed over and the three were on comfortable terms by the time supper arrived.

"Your kinsman sounds a rare steady hand," said Mr. Standeven. "So does his lady."

"Oh, she is," Alice replied. "But why do you call her his lady?"

"Ain't she? That is... I meant no disrespect to the good lady, ma'am, but from the way it sounded, I'd have fancied they were as good as engaged."

He was stumbling about to repair his mistake, and Viola found herself impressed far more favorably than if he had proved to be another of these elegant social witsnappers who were never at a loss nor ever committed a conversational blunder in the presence of her sex.

"It must have been the way I told the story," she said to help him out of his embarrassment. "It's just that they're so much alike, and both enjoy the game so well. We don't think anything about it, those of us who know 'em, but I suppose it might look a bit lovey-dovey to a stranger, in its own cold-fish way."

"But perhaps they *are* in love," murmured Alice. "Oh, Vi, I never thought of that, did you?"

"She calls me 'Vi' sometimes for 'Victor,'" young Mr. Williams informed their new acquaintance. "In honor of my illustrious namesake, you see."

"What a thing it must be to have a sister!" replied Mr. Standeven. "I can tell you my brothers' nicknames for me were nothing so kind."

"What were they, Mr. Standeven?" said Alice, clearly before thinking.

"Well...the kindest of them was 'Little Goozler.' I don't think I'd better mention the rest in polite company."

"Ah!" said Viola. "You can tell us they existed, but not what they were. Never mind, I give fair warning I'll get 'em from you when we're alone, if I have to trade you Allie's less flattering nicknames for me." (This was a promise she quite forgot when the time came.) "You've never been bullied, sir, until you've been bullied by a younger sister."

"I can't picture an unflattering name coming from Miss Williams's lips," said Mr. Standeven. "It'd turn into a compliment between her pretty teeth."

Viola waited long enough to be sure, from Alice's expression, that this speech had had its effect. Then she said, "Blather! Don't let her hoodwink you. Never trust the tongue of a young female who aspires to mold herself upon the tender Mrs. Beale."

"I do not aspire to be like Mrs. Beale!" said Alice. "She is an original. No more than you aspire to mold yourself upon Lord Spottiswood. And I have never bullied you, Caesar, it's quite the other way around."

Viola looked at Mr. Standeven and turned her eyes toward the ceiling. "There! You see it for yourself, sir."

"I've never had a sister," Standeven replied, "but since I do know what brothers are like, my friend, I'll have to sympathize with Miss Williams."

"There, yourself, Caesar!" cried Alice. "Mr. Standeven, thank you so very much for coming to my rescue. Now perhaps he won't be quite so impossible to get on with. But were you really bullied?" she added in a softer voice. "I should never have thought it."

"Only because you see me as a grown man. Unhappily, both Alfred and Thomas were several years farther along that road than I was. I think that was what made me buy my commission," he went on, letting his fork lie idle for a moment while he stared into his wineglass. "Looking for a quick, sure road to manhood. Well, Caesar, if you've any ideas about molding yourself on that victorious general your namesake, think long and hard."

The conversation had taken too serious a tone for Viola, who preferred to see her companions jocular. She thought of remarking that the prime candidate this century for the role of Julius Caesar was that Corsican devil, and what sane individual would court comparison with Bonaparte? But that did not seem likely to recapture the spirit of jest, so she changed the subject entirely, and soon had them joking and merry again, engaged in a contest of finding uncomplimentary epithets for the inn food, always a trusty if unoriginal source of wit.

Eventually they moved on to the theater. Mr. and Miss Williams described some of the most recent glories of London's dramatic and operatic stage. Mr. Standeven repaid them by reminiscing about the productions of his youth in sufficient detail to enable Viola, who remembered the older members of her circle discussing some of the same productions when she was a child, to calculate his age as between twenty-six and thirty— just right for Alice.

Mr. Standeven had himself taken part in student theatricals at Eton, had essayed both Desdemona and Iago in various performances, and floundered through the part of Iphigenia in the Greek. At their request, he whipped his memory and recited a few ringing lines for them.

At about this point, Alice took the initiative and spoke of a *George Barnwell* production that had impressed her deeply when she saw a traveling company perform it eight or nine years ago. This led to a debate on the relative merits of *George Barnwell* and St. George as Yuletide entertainment. Mr. Standeven proposed the theory that the introduction of the murderer Barnwell, where in olden times the saint and his outrageous mummery had reigned supreme, owed something to the Puritan interregnum. Viola challenged this and said she thought Barnwell's fearful example was a slightly less sanguinary method of putting forth the message otherwise conveyed by gibbeted gallow's-birds and the display of disembodied heads and quartered limbs. Alice, looking a little green over her gooseberry tart, rejoiced that an actor could play Mr. Barnwell without really being hanged, and regretted that Mr. Barnwell had not lived and died early enough for Mr. Shakespeare to have made the play out of his story.

Mr. Standeven, observing Miss Williams's sensibility to certain topics, turned the talk to some of the pleasanter customs of olden times, royal pageantries on the Thames, remarkable cakes made in the likenesses of knights, ladies, swans, and so on (which he and his brothers had once insisted their family cook try to reproduce, with disastrous results), hobbyhorses and gilt gingerbread fairings for the common folk. Alice said she had sometimes enjoyed gilt gingerbread fairings herself. Mr. Standeven inquired if she had ever sampled German goldwasser? Two or three bottles of that liquor had once come into his hands—he skirted over the exact circumstances—he had found it inferior to good sherry, but could he have seen into the future, he would have contrived to bring along one of those bottles safe in his kit against this evening, so that they might share the novelty.

The goldwasser was the nearest they came over supper to any mention of what might have been Mr. Standeven's adventures after he bought his commission in the army. Mr. Williams was in two minds about hinting that Miss Williams leave the gentlemen to their port. Viola fairly itched to have the lieutenant alone and see what martial history she could draw from him as male to male, but on the other hand she exulted in her friend's obvious reluctance to quit Mr. Standeven's company, and in his to see her go.

"Well, Mr. Standeven," Alice said with a sigh as the clock struck twelve, "who knows how slow that timepiece may be?"

"In fact, ma'am, I think they try to keep their clocks punctual in these places, what with travelers depending on 'em to be ready when the stages leave." Mr. Standeven pulled out his pocketwatch, looked at it, and closed it again as if wishing he had not consulted it. He would have tucked it away, but Viola twitched it from his hand in a gesture that would have seemed uncommon rude were it not for the easy if specious familiarity that had grown among them in the past few hours.

Viola opened the silver watchcase and grimaced. "In fact, it is almost twenty minutes after the hour. Unless Mr. Standeven's timepiece is less accurate than the Swan's, and of course nobody depends on Mr. Standeven's watch to tell 'em they must be ready for the stage."

Mr. Standeven plucked back his watch. "What time do you make it, Mr. Williams?"

"I don't. My pocketwatch was shattered a few days since," Viola lied glibly. "The fob chain broke and the instrument fell to the road where my horse trod on it." Actually, Sebastian's watch had been unavailable since he had it with him in the Lake Country, and Viola had not liked to carry her own petite, obviously feminine timepiece.

"But even if it is only just midnight," said Alice, "it's

long past time I should retire. Between two long days of travel, you know. I wish there were some way to stop the moon, as Joshua stopped the sun that time in the valley of Ajalon, because you're going on south tomorrow, are you not? and so we may never see each other again. Mr. Standeven." She extended her left hand to him.

This time he shook it. "But England's not such a lot of geography, Miss Williams. I may be in London some months. Be sure any letters left at the Officers' Mess or Smith's Bank will reach me. And after London, I should be spending most of the year at Derrydown, near Pilcroft in Kent—my own little estate, came to me from a maiden aunt, God rest her."

As Alice did not act on the hint and furnish him with her direction, Viola added, "Besides, there's no reason not to see each other again at breakfast. Mr. Standeven's riding, my dear, and so will we be, or else we'll hire a chaise, so we're none of us bound by the tyranny of anyone's timepiece."

"But Mr. Standeven may wish to make a very early start tomorrow morning." Alice had not yet withdrawn her fingers from his.

"Not after I've drunk him down tonight." Viola winked.

Alice pulled her hand away at last. "Goodnight, then, Mr. Standeven. Do be gentle with my brother, won't you? I imagine you could drink him down twenty times over, for all his boasting."

"Ma'am, I'll be as gentle with him as..." Mr. Standeven hesitated as if realizing his words might go too far, then completed the sentence anyhow: "...as I'd be with yourself, ma'am."

Alice smiled and somehow seemed to melt from the room.

"Here," said Mr. Williams, rubbing his palms together, "I don't deserve that much consideration, y'know." All those late, half-secret drinking bouts with Miss Merriweather, Noddy Duncton, and brother Basty when he could be persuaded were about to bear fruit. She felt confident in her ability to hold her liquor like any lord, and to endure a roomful of tobacco vapor too, if need be. "I do not smoke, Mr. Standeven. Got a handful of rotted weed once and it churned at my stomach for three days. Put a damper to my drinking, so I haven't risked it since."

"Quite a coincidence," said Mr. Standeven. "I got hold of a cigar once near Seville. Don't know what it'd fallen into, vinegar most like, but it ruined me for the Indian weed. I used to take snuff, but had to go without so long that I lost that habit too. It was purgatory for a while, though."

Viola wiggled her toes in Sebastian's boots. She didn't quite dare ask Standeven for the circumstances of his snuff deprivation, not just yet, but they were on the right road. "Well, sir, I hope you ain't lost your taste for drink?"

"Mr. Williams, I misdoubt there's any spot inhabited by our race on this or any other planet where a person would have to go very long without a drink of passable liquor. The old Saxons taught us how to make it out of honey, the Hollanders out of juniper berries, Polanders and Russians make it out of potatoes, Germans out of cherries and gold, Americans out of their Indian maize, Jamaicans out of molasses, Caribs out of orange peel, Lunarians probably make it out of cream cheese, and I'd not be surprised if someone somewhere can distill it from tobacco."

Viola made a face. "Meanwhile, shall we start wetting our whistles with port, punch, or brandy?"

"Milk punch. I used to mix up a rare bowl. There was nothing on shipboard but sherry or burgundy with the captain—an excellent man, but something of a Methodist—or rum and limes with the crew, so if it's to your taste, sir, I'd relish the chance to try my hand again at stirring up a bowl of my own recipe."

"Provided you let me look on and learn, I ask nothing better," said Mr. Williams.

Fortunately, the inn could furnish all the ingredients Mr. Standeven called for except pineapple, which he said was as much for decoration as flavor anyhow. Viola grew so interested in watching his one-handed dexterity that she forgot to memorize the ingredients, but the finished potation was Olympian nectar. After the first bowl, they had dropped "Mr." and were addressing each other by surname only. After the second bowl, they had progressed to "Jemmy" and "Willy."

They had not progressed to an account of the lost arm, but during that second bowl of punch Willy did learn much else of Jemmy's life and adventures. The third son of a baronet, Jemmy Standeven had joined the army in a passion of patriotism, fought the impious Corsican on the Continent, rode with stout comrades and good friends until at last he was left for dead on the field and stripped clean by battlefield robbers while unconscious. Awaking naked near dawn, he had crawled to a hut where the peasants nursed him and clad him in the remnants of a French uniform, doubtless stolen from another lifeless soldier. He had made his way to Lisbon, unable to find any of his own countrymen but sometimes having to dodge enemy troops who might have mistook him for a deserter and would have held him prisoner even if they believed his story. He had passed an indeterminate time in Lisbon, soothed and further nursed by the kindest and cleanest public woman he had ever met—not, he added, that he'd ever had any extensive dealings with her kind as a whole, but Albina should have been born to better things, and he was glad to remember that at the same time she was favoring him she'd been in the way of cajoling a Portuguese landowner into marrying her. Before he could see the wedding, however, he had been laid on by thieves in a dark alley and wakened aboard a Russian whaling ship, where they forced him to help kill a whale or two before he could pick up enough of the language to persuade the Russian captain to let him be transferred to an English vessel. He was fortunate that the captain of the first English vessel they came across, a merchantman, was willing to ransom a ragged fellow Briton on the promise of future repayment. The English ship was now being unloaded in her home port of Liverpool, and Standeven, having borrowed clothes from her officers and made a short detour through Wigan and Manchester to cash a draft for his travel expenses on the captain's preferred banker and partially return these favors by transmitting a few messages of business or personal nature, was hurrying to London to collect his back pay, tender his resignation from the Guards, search out old friends who must think him long dead, and, he hoped, find his affairs still sufficiently in order that he could draw a draft on his own banker for the sum the English captain had paid the Russian on his behalf.

"Good thing, that, you was able to pick up their queer lingo," said Viola, whose tongue was by now beginning to feel slightly uneasy around her own language.

"Not so hard as you might think, Willy. The Russian gab's pretty much like the Polanders'. Once I caught that, I could follow some of it pretty well. Had a harder time trying to speak it, o' course. Couldn't get rid of my nasals—'um's' and 'an's' and 'om's.' Had to learn 'em so thorough for French, y'see, and the Poles use 'em about as freely as the French, but the Russians don't.

Some of those sailors must still think I was a Polander or a Frenchman."

"D'ye speak Polish, then?"

"A little. Learned it from my chum Modrowski. Captured him at...at..." Standeven shrugged. "All these battles start t' run together after a couple of years."

"It's your punch. Here's to Shtandev...Shtand ...Jemmy's milk punch!" Viola drank off the last of it in her toast. "Some plain, hot negush to clear our heads?"

He shook his. "Port. It's simpler. Only need t' pour it."

"Pour port!" Viola giggled and rang for the potboy.

"Good old Count Modrowski," Standeven mused on as they waited for bottles of port and madeira. "Excellent fellow. Never would give his parole—rather keep his honor free to escape and fight again. Hot for Boney. But an excellent fellow for all that."

"Contradicshun in terms."

The spirits were delivered. Standeven uncorked a bottle one-handed and poured port. "Political difference is all. Like religion. You find good Baptists, good papists, good Methodists, good atheists, why not good Bonapartists?"

Viola shook her head, less at Standeven's argument than at his continued ability to pronounce all those sibilants. She resolved to drink her port more leisurely. "What became of your Polander count?"

Standeven shrugged. "Still in England, I suppose, if he's not escaped. Hope t' get word of him, too, when I get to London. Be good to shake him by the hand again...." His voice trailed off as he gazed at his left fingers around the stem of the wineglass.

Excess of spirits and the lateness of the hour had finally dulled Viola's caution. "Cannonball?" she asked, following his gaze.

The same factors at work upon her seemed also to have blunted some of his tenderness on the subject. "No. Whale line. Got a harpoon rope twisted around it out in the whaleboat." He shrugged. "Maybe made that Russian captain just as willing t' be rid of me, after all."

And since that had been the evening's most pressing problem in Viola's mind, her head was more full of whaleboats and rushing oceans than of Polish counts when at last, however reluctantly, she removed her person from the table in time to save herself from slipping beneath it.

She wove her way to Alice's room. The candle was out, but the small fire was still glowing, and Alice was lying awake, for she called out softly, "Caesar?"

"Willy. Willy for Williams." Reflecting on her access of new names, Viola groped to the bed, gave her friend a résumé of Mr. Standeven's adventures and how he had lost his arm, and recommended that Alice meet him at breakfast tomorrow. "You'll have him alone the whole time. I don't think I'll be up before afternoon."

"You shall be up by nine," said Alice, "for while you two were at your boozing I had the most horrible nightmare about Grandfather—or else it was Father—catching us up with the Bow Street runners and some...some pugilists, I think."

Viola moaned. "Ten o'clock. Not before. Your grandfather might bring runners, but he wouldn't bring pushilishts."

"And Mr. Standeven may be in as sad condition as you are in the morning, and not desirous of any conversation at all."

"Doubt it. Wear your muslin and look bright and pretty. Damme, but he can hold his liquor. He could shtill get out his shib— His curly letters, you know."

All this vital information carefully communicated,

Viola sought her own bed and dreamed of nothing for hours until, in the bleary dawn, she half opened her eyes and saw a large, nonexistent gray whale in bed with her. Too tired to push it out, she ignored it and slept again, to the accompaniment of little, scumbering mice who kept sticking bayonets and harpoons into various strategic points of her cranium.

Chapter 10.

Whilst Viola was dreaming the gray whale out of her bed again, Alice had risen, washed her face and hands, put on her spotted muslin traveling frock, combed her golden curls with special care, compressed a clean handkerchief into her reticule, and made her way to last night's parlor, where they had arranged, before the spirits started flowing so freely, that an early breakfast would be laid for them. Judging what Mr. Standeven's condition was likely to be from what Viola's had been, Alice feared she would breakfast alone; but she determined to linger over her rolls and coffee until their new acquaintance appeared, if she had to breakfast till nuncheon. Such a bold-faced scheme made her conscience blush furiously, and it was a moot point whether she could have sat to her guns for more than half an hour before her staid upbringing routed the opportunity of a lifetime.

But to her mingled relief and dismay, she found Mr. Standeven already in the parlor, as if awaiting her.

"Miss Williams, ma'am," he said, rising and making his bow at once on her entrance. "I trust you slept well?"

It was the exact question she had rehearsed greeting

him with, but she had not rehearsed the answer. "Oh...ah...very well, sir. And you?"

"Dreamlessly."

He's come much better prepared, she thought. He has foreseen all possible circumstances and rehearsed accordingly. Or perhaps all gentlemen are at their ease so soon as they've decided a lady is not really worth deeper acquaintance.

Meanwhile, Mr. Standeven was asking her whether she preferred tea or coffee. She gave her vote almost at random, he poured, and she did not realize until the second or third sip that she had preferred tea this morning.

"But 'dreamlessly' may be good or bad, sir, may it not?" she said. "That is, very good if you slept without any bad dreams, but rather disappointing not to have had any pleasant ones." Oh, she thought, I could have said that very wittily, if I had polished it beforehand.

He refilled his own cup with both coffee and tea and added sugar. "That's very true, ma'am. But I find there's usually a sort of stammer between when things happen and when I start to dream about them. I should start having some very pleasant dreams in about three or four nights now." Then, as if he had said something a little too forward, he looked down at the twist he was stirring round and round in his cup. "I've had bad dreams for so long now, you see, that when I said I had a dreamless sleep of it last night, I meant it was good."

"Oh. I'm sorry. Are they very terrible nightmares?" I'm probing at his past, she scolded herself, biting her tongue.

"Well, not nightmares so much...I conceive a dream can be less than pleasant without quite earning the name of a nightmare."

"Mr. Derrywinkle—our curate at home, you see—calls nightmares the mark of a sinful conscience." Alice

109

bit her tongue again and hastened to explain her true moral: "But I think that must be humbug! After all, who wakes up oftener screaming from bad dreams than little children, who are much too young to have any such sins on their conscience?"

"Then you don't subscribe to the old idea of infant damnation, ma'am?"

"No, sir, I do not. I think it is a perfectly stupid doctrine. That is..." (Oh, my, we're both forgetting our shyness now, she thought, and with the thought her shyness naturally returned.) "That is, I haven't any degree, of course, but do you know, I think I must have read almost as much divinity as some of the preachers I've heard speak."

He nodded. "From what I've heard, the Wesleyans and the dissenters preach the best. I think I've heard that in Quakerism the women preach as well as the men."

There followed half an hour of doctrinal debate in which the participants did forget their bashfulness in discovering that they were both half dissenters themselves, and that many of their points of dissent from High Church doctrine followed remarkably similar lines.

"Of course," he remarked at last, "the only Protestant preacher I've heard in more than a year was the chaplain on board the *Pride of Liverpool,* and more often than not he put me to sleep before I could get the gist of his sermons."

That brought Alice back to self-consciousness. "The *Pride of Liverpool?*" She felt as if every drop of blood had drained from her head and was fighting to rush back up.

"Aye—is anything wrong, Miss Williams?"

"The *Pride of Liverpool?* You're sure?" Could it have been two years already? She made a rapid mental cal-

110

culation. "She was not to have docked for at least three months yet! I—I have a friend who has a...a brother aboard, you see."

"Ah? What's his name? I came to know most of the men pretty well."

"In matter of fact...it was the chaplain."

"Well, well!" Mr. Standeven smiled, but the smile changed to a puzzled frown. "Dr. Stubbins? But he's in his sixties and I thought he was the last of his clan."

Oh, dear, thought Alice, what a stupid mistake! "His brother in religion, I meant—our Reverend Mr. Derrywinkle, you see. But they were not to dock for three or four months yet. Is anything—has anything happened?"

He smiled again and shook his head. "Rest easy, ma'am, they didn't lose a hand, made most of their scheduled ports, and came home with a good cargo. Maybe not quite so good as they'd hoped, but enough to turn a tidy profit. I'm afraid I'm partly to blame. Captain Markham was kind enough to cut his trip a little short and get me back to England as soon as possible."

"Oh," she said. "Oh..." Tears were starting in her eyes. She could not help it. She always cried with relief each time her father came home safe; and now when her natural relief was mixed with equally natural fear, guilt, regret that she could not have welcomed him in innocence...Could she find some excuse for dabbing at her eyes, so as not to rouse Mr. Standeven's suspicion? She fumbled for her handkerchief. It caught on something at the mouth of the reticule. She pulled it free with so hard a jerk that reticule and all fell with a plop to the floor beneath the table. She bent down and bumped her head.

Whilst she was rubbing it, thinking fuzzily that this would explain her tears, Mr. Standeven retrieved her

111

things. He returned the reticule at once, but something about the handkerchief caught his eye. To her horror, she remembered that it was embroidered with the initial of her last name!

"*M?*" he said. "Miss Williams?"

"*W!* It's a *W!*" She snatched the handkerchief from his hand.

"That's a *W?*"

"The—the embroideress had the pattern upside down. If you'll pardon me, sir..." She rose and ran from the room, hoping he might charge her haste to the several cups of tea she had drunk.

She flew, stumbling, to Viola's room, through the door (just remembering to shut it again behind her), and half fell upon the bed. "Vi! Vi! Oh, Caesar!"

Viola pushed at her and turned over. Alice tried shaking, then pommeling. "Caesar! Caesar! Vi—oh, I'll start calling you something else very soon!"

The sleeper woke at last, hitched herself up on the bolster, and stared at her friend. "Eleven o'clock already?"

"No, it is..." Alice tried to recollect what the parlor clock had said. "I think it's half past nine, but the most terrible thing! Oh, Vi, it was the *Pride of Liverpool* brought Mr. Standeven home."

Viola squinted and brushed at the pillows. "I'm sorry, Allie, I ain't quite sure whether there was mice in bed with me or whether they were a dream, too. Well, what's this terrible thing that's just happened at half past nine in the morning?"

Alice dropped her voice to an urgent near-whisper. "Viola, the *Pride of Liverpool!* My father's ship!"

Viola slapped the pillow and whistled softly. "Well," she said, "but Captain Markham didn't come along with him, anyhow. So let's have the whole story, my dear, who knows what and how did they learn it?"

Alice poured out the whole tale in all its fearsome details. The recital took more time than the event had done. Viola listened soberly, though still picking at threads in the bedclothes.

"Right," said Viola when she had heard the Awful Disclosure through to the end. "I'd have made up a better story about the handkerchief. You might've said it was a rag we'd found on the road and washed and mended, or a keepsake from a friend or an inheritance from an aunt. But still, it's not so bad. He don't really know anything, and he might swallow that about your embroideress getting the pattern upside down—"

"He won't! It was just too stupid, and now he's sure to see the likeness between Father's features and mine, everyone always remarks how much I take after my father."

"People see those things when they're looking for them. Standeven won't be looking. Not because of a silly *M* on your handkerchief. Why, half the names in the world must begin with *M*."

"That is stupid," said Alice.

"Yes, but a good many of 'em do, anyhow. Standeven was telling me only last night about some Polander...Modernski, Modesski..." Viola shrugged. "The point is, he can't know, and whatever he may suspect, if anything at all, you're the only one who could've put it into his head. Now, he's on his way to London with a great deal of business of his own. I conceive it can't be simple to get your affairs back in order if everyone has been thinking you dead for a year or two. And Captain Markham stopped in Liverpool seeing to his cargo—Standeven told me that much last night, now I think of it—"

"Viola! You knew last night?"

"Not names. Or not to remember, anyhow. But your father will still be in Liverpool..."

"Unless he's gone home to Markham House already."

"Well, what if he has? Our people won't have guessed he's docked, so they won't have written to him about us. So we still have several days clear, nothing to worry about except Cousin Launcelot and Mrs. Beale. Maybe we'd better not go through Manchester now, though." Viola frowned. "We'll have to cut across to the Glasgow road at...fetch me *Kearsley's Guide* from the table there, will you? The devil! And I was looking forward to seeing Knock-castle, and the old wall at Castlefield. I hope we don't meet my guardian prematurely on the Glasgow road."

"But what are we to do in the meantime? About poor Mr. Standeven waiting in the parlor, and maybe suspecting..."

"Yes, that's the worst of it, your rushing out like that. Well, you'll have to go down to him and see he don't suspect, of course."

"Oh, but..."

Viola sighed. "Oh, very well. I'll dress and go make your excuses to him for you. You can hide in our rooms and pack up my things for me. But see you don't wad them all into wrinkles this time."

So Caesar Williams dressed despite the lingering ache in his head and went to tell Standeven that his sister had suddenly took ill—nothing serious or alarming, just a female complaint, you know—while Miss Williams packed in the bedrooms, feeling almost as faint and headachy as her supposed brother was describing her, although for different reasons.

Mr. Williams breakfasted and joked a bit with Mr. Standeven, who sat on over a few more cups of twist to bear the younger fellow company and, perhaps, to take a more regular leave of Miss Williams if she rejoined them. She did not, and her brother was forced to look in on her after breakfast so as to reassure Standeven again there was no cause for alarm. They went together to see what horses were available for hire. Fortunately, the situation was better in Leek than Standeven had found it in Macclesfield, and he chose a mettlesome roan stallion called Swisher to continue his journey south. Mr. Williams bespoke a well-hung curricle and pair of gentle amblers named Tilly and Milly, giving Standeven his guarantee that he would drive them at an easy pace, and not set out until Miss Williams felt up to it, even if that took until tomorrow morning.

Mr. Williams stood in the innyard and waved as Standeven rode away, and Miss Williams strained to catch a glimpse of him from the window. Then Mr. Williams changed his plan about the curricle and amblers, hired instead a couple of likely saddle ponies named Tatches and Netty, and within another quarter hour Mr. and Miss Williams were cantering cross-country to the Glasgow road.

Chapter 11.

Two days before, Lord Spottiswood had returned from arranging with a good Hatfield wheelwright to see to Viola's broken cabriolet, and found Mrs. Beale sitting alone in the private parlor of the Salisbury Arms, reading a tattered inn copy of Locke's *Essay Concerning Human Understanding* (the letters being finished but for his lordship's signature, and Sir Toby being marched up and down the walk by Mr. Duncton and Miss Merriweather in an effort to work off some of his fidgets).

Mrs. Beale had put down the book and said to Lord Spottiswood, "It has occurred to me that they may well plan to hide in the country home of Alice's father, Captain Markham, between Manchester and Liverpool."

"Since it would appear that no young man is involved," replied Lord Spottiswood, "I would calculate your thought to have a considerably greater factor of probability than that they are aiming for Gretna Green."

So instead of continuing on Kearsley's recommended road from London to Glasgow by way of Boroughbridge, Carlisle, and Gretna Green, they struck back at their earliest convenience to the Manchester road. Driving until even Sir Toby was willing to make a halt for the night, they reached Northampton. A series of minor annoyances and mishaps, largely happening at the inns and posthouses where they stopped for light refreshment and a change of horses (and largely, perhaps, traceable to Noddy Duncton or Agnes Merriweather, if the others had spent more time for thorough investigation) had prevented their getting farther than Derby the next day. Nevertheless, they had spent the night less than thirty miles from the Swan with Two Necks, contrary to Viola's blithe assumption that her guardian's party should be between Newark and Doncaster on the Glasgow road by now.

Between Derby and Leek, Lord Spottiswood's party stopped to refresh itself, on Miss Merriweather's urgent insistence, at the Red Lion. Between Leek and Derby, Mr. Standeven stopped to rest his horse at the same inn.

Noddy Duncton made first contact. Rubbing shoulders with the former military man in the taproom, Noddy proposed a game of dominoes, with a view to prolong his own respite from travel and help insure Viola all the time she needed. Moreover, he thought, there was always the very thin chance that Spotty would be sufficiently annoyed on finding him squandering half an hour like this to give him a dressing-down that would win his wager.

But it was Mrs. Beale who came at last into the taproom and found them. Duncton suspected Merriweather's hand in this, but Merriweather was foiled again, for on seeing what was afoot, the magnificent Beale said quietly, "Dominoes provide an excellent mathematical pastime, Mr. Duncton, and I'm sure you may stand a better chance with his lordship at that game than at chess. But meanwhile, sir," she went on, turning to Standeven, "I fear circumstances force us to take away your opponent."

Duncton rose to the occasion. "Mrs. Beale, allow me to present Mr. Standeven, late of the Royal Horse Guards. Mr. Standeven, our esteemed friend Mrs. Matthew Beale of London and Islington."

"Mr. Standeven." Without embarrassment or hesitation, she extended her left hand for his shake.

"Your devoted, ma'am. I hope the pressing circumstances are pleasant rather than otherwise. I think I was about to beat your friend roundly at this pastime."

Mrs. Beale shook her head. "Mr. Duncton, is there no game you can master?" Then, to Standeven, "Do you travel north or south, sir?"

"To London, ma'am. If you're traveling the same road, and wouldn't object to another companion, I'd be honored to match my pace to your party's."

"Unfortunately, we are traveling north. Mr. Duncton seems to have been very discreet with you. I shall be less so. Have you in your journey south seen or heard of two young ladies, probably traveling alone, one about my own height and very slender, with brown hair which may or may not still be in curls, and a complexion sufficiently brunette to verge on the unfashionable; the other somewhat shorter and plumper, with bright yellow ringlets, gray eyes, and a very pale skin."

Mr. Standeven started perceptibly.

Drat! thought Duncton, If he was so shocked as that at their traveling *sans* chaperon, he'd have jumped before the description. He's seen 'em, right enough.

"I...I haven't seen nor heard of your young ladies, ma'am," said Standeven. "But I just left—no, it has to be coincidence—I just left a young lady traveling with her brother, a Miss and Mr. Williams, and she could answer your second description perfect, except I'd have called her eyes blue."

118

"Well," said Mrs. Beale, "I imagine there are more young women of that general description than one might suppose."

"They're thick as grass," Duncton put in hopefully. "Plays, poems, paintings, songs, novels—all full of 'em, and the authors had to get the idea from somewhere, y'know."

But Mrs. Beale was examining the suspicion rationally, not rejecting it. "Nevertheless, Mr. Standeven, though blue-eyed, golden-haired maidens may tumble from the branches of life into those of literature by the hundred whenever the tree is shook, I think perhaps I had best beg you to join the rest of our party and expand a little on the details of your meeting with Miss and Mr. Williams."

So Standeven accompanied Mrs. Beale and Duncton to the private parlor where the rest of their party were taking refreshment. Introductions effected, he sat with them and told them how, stopping last night at the Swan with Two Necks in Leek, he had made the acquaintance first of Mr. Williams, then of Miss Williams, who so nearly fit Mrs. Beale's description of one of the young ladies they were after.

"Fascinating," said Lord Spottiswood.

"So there *is* a rascally seducer in it, after all," said Miss Merriweather, "and all your fine theory about our girls just running off together for a little lark, as you've been foisting off on Sir Toby here, is so much wind!"

But this effort perturbed only Sir Toby, who choked on the toast and tea which was all the late-morning sustenance they had attempted to get into him.

Spottiswood cut a few more slices of cheese for his bread and inquired, "Can you describe Mr. Williams?"

"Well..." Standeven seemed a little less clear about the young man's features, as if the young lady's had impressed him the more. "Not so tall as me, but not too

119

shortish. Taller than his sister, anyhow. Narrowish shoulders. Dark hair...I can't recollect the color of his eyes."

"Lean or fleshy?" said Mrs. Beale.

"Lean," Standeven replied, and then looked slightly puzzled about it.

Spottiswood and Mrs. Beale exchanged glances. So did Duncton and Miss Merriweather. Sir Toby blubbered into his tea that his sweet little girl was ruined by a seducing fortune hunter and if he didn't call the blackguard out himself, old as he was, and have his false heart out of his body, his son Robert Markham would.

Standeven jumped to his feet. "The handkerchief! Ma'ams, sirs, Miss Williams had a handkerchief embroidered with *M*. She claimed it was a *W* done upside down by mistake, but it was an *M*, or I never rode a horse. Gods, if he ain't her brother..."

"They have not yet reached Gretna Green," said Spottiswood, "and if you left them in Leek this morning, there is a high probability that we will overtake them before they do."

"Will you drink a cup of tea or mug of ale with us, Mr. Standeven," said Mrs. Beale, "or must you leave us already?"

"Aye, and why shouldn't he leave us?" said Miss Merriweather. "What's Alice to him, or he to our Alice?"

Standeven sat down again. Unaccountably, he was quivering a little. "By God, if that's the way of it, Sir Toby, you won't need to wait for your son. I'll call the scoundrel out for you myself, youngster or not."

"Thought you was on your way to London?" Duncton put in.

"Some matters come first. If you'll allow my help? God, Captain Markham's daughter, too..."

Spottiswood was chewing a mouthful of bread and cheese.

Miss Merriweather said, "If the rapscallion's a mere green younker, a good, sound thrashing'll be our best course."

"Thrashing!" Sir Toby brought his fist down on the table with enough force to rattle the crockery. "He's ruined her, I tell you! Here's four men of us here, and if one of us ain't the man to stop his breath..."

Lord Spottiswood took a draught of ale. "If I countenanced the barbaric custom of dueling, I should incline to agree with you. A youth old enough to persuade a well-bred lady to this rash adventure is old enough to be chastised for it as an adult. Mr. Standeven, I assume that young Mr. Williams has a Christian name. Did he furnish you with it?"

"Caesar."

"Caesar." Spottiswood exchanged another glance with Mrs. Beale. "You recall Shakespeare's *Twelfth Night?*"

"In some detail," she replied, "though I prefer *Midsummer Night's Dream.* I also recall that the bard's Christian name was William."

His lordship nodded. "I postulate that our most intelligent course of action will be first to find them and only then to select our correctional measures."

Chapter 12.

Viola and Alice reached Doncaster too late, or at least too tired, to shop for any of the knit stockings and gloves which were the town's principal manufacture, but not too late to view the ruinous castle in the long rosy light of a clear evening more than a thousand years after lightning had fired the venerable pile. Viola began to compose an ode. Alice suggested that if they were going no farther that night, they ought to choose an inn.

They chose the Rein Deer, bespoke rooms, and Alice went upstairs at once to rest a little and change her dress before supper. Viola, more excited than exhausted by the quirks of the day, took advantage of her male attire to lounge in the taproom with a tankard of ale, meditate on her ode to the ruined castle, and watch the local custom and stagecoach travelers about her.

The taproom was not crowded tonight. Small knots of talkers sent up a murmuration rather than a din, punctuated by guffaws of laughter or argument and by snatches loud enough to follow for a few moments without straining your ears overhard to filter one dialogue from the rest. Tobacco smoke, more pleasing to the eyes than the nostrils, remained thin enough not to suffocate, but curled about in romantic spectre-shapes and occasional rings, half making Viola wish that she, too, had a pipe at which to puff away and look wise.

Eventually, however, she tired of the lone observer's role and glanced about for some acquaintance to strike up. At first it looked unpromising. Most of the folk were already tight in conversation with their own little cliques, while the solitary drinkers tended to an uncouth, dour and forbidding appearance.

But there was one gentlemen, at a table in a far corner.... Viola examined him as closely as she could across the length of the room in the gloaming. He seemed young enough (for a male) and handsome. He had supped—the dishes were shoved to the other side of his table awaiting the servant—and he sat with his glass of port and a lighted candle before him, toying with...a pack of cards?

Viola took her half-emptied tankard and crossed the room to his table. While her approach was not furtive, she did come up softly and to one side, so that for a while he continued his pastime in seeming unawareness that she watched over his shoulder.

He shuffled the pack and began laying the cards on the table, aces down the center, the rest in eight rows, four to the right and four to the left, each new card overlapping the one before it in its row. When he turned up the deuces, he put them square atop the aces, and one trey, that was almost the last card, he laid square on its deuce. When he had all the cards arranged before him, he began to move the ones at the ends around from row to row, a seven on an eight, a knave on a queen....

Viola walked from behind his shoulder to the empty chair at the other side of his table. He looked up at her with the trace of a smile.

He was extraordinary handsome. His face was lean,
123

forehead high, eyes immense and dark and lustrous, nose straight and delicate in its strength, chin cleft. His hair looked black and his skin deep olive in the fading twilight. There was a tiny scar on his right cheek, more like an old-fashioned beauty patch than a disfigurement.

This wonderful face showed no surprise—something like indulgence instead—so she guessed he had been aware of her approach but taken it as calmly as Cousin Launcelot would have done. She remembered she was a young man and therefore need display no hesitation. She sat in the chair opposite the stranger, took a deep pull from her tankard, wiped her mouth on her sleeve, pushed the dirty supper dishes out of her line of vision, and gestured at the cards. "Are you a gypsy, fellow?" His complexion was dark enough, his features sufficiently romantic. "Is that how you spread out your cards to read the future in 'em?"

His smile faded and he shook his head. "No. I am not a gypsy. I am a Polander."

"Oh." The last sentence explained his mild accent. It also reminded her of something, but she could not remember what. She hadn't meant to offend him, but his handsomeness made her brusque. "Pity, that, in its way. I was about to have you read my fortune."

"This is not fortune-reading. I am good Catholic. This is a pastime. A game one plays against one's self."

"Really? What's the purpose of such a game?"

"It is like when one sets the chessboard and plays both colors, now black, now white." He spoke as if he had had to explain it more than once to other people. "That, too, is a game one plays against one's self."

"No, it ain't. Not exactly. That's to sharpen your wits for a real game, work out problems."

"And this also is to work out problems. You see, here is the fortress." He pointed to the row of aces, three of them blanketed with deuces and one with a trey. "And here is the army." He pointed to the rows of overlapping cards to right and left. "The army must find weak places in the defense, strike, and breach the walls." By transferring an eight to a nine and a six to a seven in various rows, he uncovered a four and moved it to the trey in the central column.

"Then what are the deuces and trey you put on the aces while you was laying your army out?"

"The spies, I think. Or perhaps the... *quel est*... the pioneers."

"You must be a military man, eh?"

"Ah." He smiled, and Viola's toes curled a little in her brother's boots. "I was, but no longer," he went on, gathering up the cards. "I am a country gentleman now. You will allow me to show you a game that is like a country dance?" He arranged the four queens in a sort of compass-rose design, laid the fives and sixes in a circle around them, shuffled the rest of the pack and began turning cards up one at a time, playing them up or down on the fives and sixes as pips matched and numbers fell in sequence. Viola watched intrigued, noticing that for all his obvious skill at the curious pastime, his hands trembled as if he were a little nervous.

If I were dressed as myself, she thought, I'd be delighted to make him nervous. But why should he react this way to a beardless youth?

The Polander finished his game and spread his hands above the tableau. "There. It is like the quadrille dance. *n'est-ce pas?*"

He slips rather easily into French, thought Viola, ignoring the fact that under the right circumstances she sometimes did so herself. Aloud, she asked, "How many patterns of this sort of trick d'ye have at your fingers' ends?"

"At my fingers' ends..." he repeated slowly. "Ah!

Four, maybe five. We play them much in Poland. We call them *La Patience*."

"Sounds more like French than Polish."

"We learn French from our childhood. It is *la langue internationale, n'est-ce pas?* The language polite and social?" He gathered the pack together again and held it out to her. "You wish to try?"

"*La Patience,* eh? Well, why not?" Viola took and shuffled the cards. "What was that first one, the one with the fortress and the besieging army?"

Growing up with Lord Spottiswood for a cousin and guardian had taught her enough skill of observation that she could begin laying down the cards as she had seen the Polander do, and, cards being the double-headed representations they were, he was able to guide her play from across the table as well as if he had been sitting beside or standing behind her. It was a simple game to master, and as she moved the last king to the last queen and picked up the cards to reshuffle them she said, "Now this time you'll have t' let me play it out with no help."

He gave her another of his half-shy smiles. "I must sit quiet and say nothing? Neither in French nor in English? Nor even Polish that you would hear and not comprehend?"

"No, I didn't say that. Don't say anything about *La Patience,* but talk about anything else you like. You can get us another round of drinks, for instance. I'll have sherry. I ain't supped yet." Viola put down the column of aces. "And then you can tell me somewhat about your military career."

"The drinks, yes." He raised his arm to summon the tapboy. "But you will not like to hear about my military career."

She bridled. Even when she went in female garb, she was accustomed to persuading men almost at once that she could listen to tales of blood and cannonfire with the stoutest of them. "What d'ye take me for, some queasy schoolboy? The more action, the better I'll like it! Here, I'll lay you a guinea to half a crown I can play this *Patience* through and listen to your bloodiest battlefield story at the same time without missing a play."

"No. It is that I was an enemy. You good English do not like to hear stories all of French courage."

"Leave out the French courage and just give me your own. I never heard yet of the soldier who didn't like to boast a bit," said Viola, conveniently forgetting the trouble she had had only last night in drawing some of Standeven's history from him.

The tapboy came, took the dirty dishes and went to fetch the second round of drinks. The Polander resumed, "If we drink together, we should make our introductions, *n'est-ce pas?* I am August, Count Modrowski, your servant." He held out his strong-looking right hand.

Where have I heard that name? thought Viola. "How d'ye spell it?" she asked.

"Exactly as you say it. M-O-D-R-O-W-S-K-I." He spoke as if he had explained it often.

"Count Modrowski," she repeated, taking his hand. "And my name's Williams. Caesar Williams, Esquire, at your service." His fingers were as strong as they looked, but she thought she returned pressure for pressure pretty handily. "Well, Count, do you take up my wager, or not?"

He shook his head. "You see, I do not like to speak of my military career because *l'Empereur* comes into the talk always."

"And you don't like talking about the Corsican butcher. I can't fault you for that. Still, all in all, courage is courage in friend or foe, so leave out the politics and just give me the battles."

He had looked about to interrupt, but taken some deep breaths instead. Only when she finished speaking did he reply. "But *l'Empereur* is not butcher. He is great and glorious man. To cry aloud his praise, I would be proud."

"What? That wretch? That atheistical monster?"

"This is why I do not like to speak of him."

Modrowski—Standeven's chum! she thought. Standeven's prisoner of war...but what else was it he told me about him? Aloud, she said, "Well, I suppose there's two sides to every fight, or not even the Frenchers would follow him. So what's your side to it, Modrowski?"

"Polska—Poland—our homeland, our beautiful homeland, our country who saved Europe from the Turks at Vienna—she is torn apart, quartered up into pieces. Russia here, Prussia here—" he positioned his wineglass and the candlestick for Russia and Prussia. "Here Austria." He looked around for a piece to represent the third offending nation and seized on her nearly empty tankard of ale. "The Emperor Napoleon is our hope. He will free us, join our Poland again from Baltic to *Karpackie*—Carpathian Mountains—from east of Vistula to west of Oder, all where are her true and natural boundaries. *L'Empereur* will give us back our Poland, our *chevalier* of all the nations."

"Well, that last comes it a bit strong. After all, Britannia's something of a *chevalier* among nations too, ain't she?" (What *was* it Standeven told me about this fellow?)

Modrowski sat back in his chair and forced a smile. "Of course. You love Britannia as I love Poland. Each loves their own homeland. But Britannia is not torn up into little pieces, you see."

"And how d'ye know *l'Empereur* is going to keep all his fine promises?"

128

"There is the Duchy of Warsaw, is there not? Already he has give us back the heart for our Poland. So far he has kept his *parole,* his word of honor you see, and with the victories that come..."

Parole, thought Viola. Word of honor...

Having let his voice trail off as if realizing he went too far, the count shook his head and resumed, "If you English could see this...this vision for the future, if you could join us and not fight...but it is your leaders, and to each their loyalty. Ah! Our second round of drinks."

Sure enough, the tapboy had come up to leave glasses of port and sherry and collect coins for the same. Modrowski paid, including a *quelque chose pour boire* that turned the boy's slight frown (probably inspired by the snatches of political jabber he must have overheard) into a grin.

Meanwhile, Viola remembered: His parole! Standeven said that Modrowski would never give his word to stay in England—that he hoped to escape and fight again. And here he is wandering free about the north of England! He *has* escaped—he's on his way to join Boney's troops. And with what he's learned here, hobnobbing with all those trusting, good-fellow officers— if Standeven's a fair example...

Modrowski turned back to her, smiled, and lifted his glass. "To honor. And to the fair, free world of the future."

Viola lifted her glass and echoed the toast. This time hers was the hand that trembled. She took a longer sip than necessary and said, "So what is it you're doing now, Count?"

"I septentrionate."

"You what?"

He looked taken aback. "I journey north. It is a good English word, is it not?"

"Oh. Uh, yes. From the Latin, I think. 'I journey north' would do just as well, though." Thinking he seemed crestfallen, she hurried to add, "And why are you septentrionating? What calls you north, hey?"

"Land. I am a country gentleman now," he boasted. "I go to see my new estate."

"Eh, what?" She thought, he's already choosing what parcel he'll beg when Boney cuts England up! "Well, here's to your new English estate." She drained off the rest of her sherry. It might not have been wise to pour even so little as a tankard of strong ale and a glass of middling sherry into a stomach that had received no food since an afternoon hunch of bread and cheese at a friendly farmhouse, but now the young Englishwoman glimpsed her duty clear. Enemy spies were enemy spies, and all the more dangerous when they were thrillingly handsome and passionately persuasive in their own patriotism. "So," she went on, "you septentrionate to mark out a pretty piece of land, and then on to Hull or Tynemouth and ship back to Boney, hey? Or will it be to Liverpool and across to the bloody Irish?"

"I beg your pardon?" he said, frowning. "You speak very fast."

"Aye, too fast for your foreigner's ears, I'll wager." She slowed her speech to a patronizing deliberation. "I inquired—asked—if you are going to sneak away and serve your Corsican devil on the Continent or in Ireland."

Some of the others in the taproom were watching them now.

"You are wrong, Mr. Williams," said Modrowski (but his scowl convinced her she was right). "I stay now in England. I win this land playing at cards, and I stay here until I can go home with peace."

"Count," she said, "I beg to tell you you're an atrocious liar."

The wineglass snapped in his hand.

He'll call me out now, sure, she thought, with one fleeting regret that she had not shouted to the room at large while she had an honorable chance to summon assistance.

But Modrowski wiped his fingers with his handkerchief, breathed hard, and said, "Young Englishman, you are patriot. You do not like my company. Go."

"Aye, lad," said one of the lookers-on. "I've rode with 'im from Scarthing Moor. He's got papers—"

"Oh. Papers." The man who had spoke up in Modrowski's defense was a low, unshaven codger who smelled of onions, and this did nothing to lay Viola's suspicion. Papers could be forged. "Why, that makes everything tight and shipshape, *n'est-ce pas?*" She stood and shouted for the tapboy. "Another round! Your best French cognac brandy this time, and we'll drink to honor amongst Bonapartists."

Modrowski stood up, ugly in his anger. "Look you. Your country is torn—bleeding—" he used a grinding Polish word and scattered the cards of her *Patience.* "Like that! How do you—"

"You've ruined my game," said Viola. "Sir, name your weapons!"

"I do not fight duels!" he shouted.

"And I do!" she shouted back. "Name your weapons, sir!"

"Sir George has a prime set of pistols," another bystander added helpfully. "I've tried 'em once. Balance perfect, triggers that jump to your touch."

Count Modrowski sat again, wiping his forehead with his handkerchief, forgetful that it was soaked with port wine. A few splinters of glass must have got into the cloth as well. He did not seem to notice it was smearing his face with more moisture than had beaded there before, but suddenly he uttered a short excla-

131

mation and snatched it away to reveal a spot of blood starting to well up above his right brow.

"I do not fight duels," he repeated. "I am a brave man. I have fought in many battles. I do not need to prove my courage, fighting in duel with an unbearded boy."

"Beardless boy," Viola corrected. "Count, you add insult. You're no man of honor or courage if you deny me the right to prove my courage upon you."

He balled up his handkerchief in one hand, then began twisting it to shreds. Drops of port fell to the table. "I will not fight."

"Here," said the helpful bystander, apparently local gentry, who knew Sir George. "Give the lad his chance."

A murmur went through the room. Viola could not tell if sympathy ran higher against the foreign Bonapartist or the rude young man who baited so obviously and unmercifully; but in any case, the company was naturally keen for a cockfight.

Count Modrowski looked around and sighed. "We will need seconds."

"Done!" said the helpful bystander.

They both looked at him. "Well, fine," said Viola. "Thanks for your help, old son, but for which of us d'ye prefer to act?"

"Either one o' you." He rubbed his hands. "Both, if you like. Your choice, gentlemen."

"I think," said the count, "this is a man who likes to see bloodspill. I know such before."

"Capital!" Viola got to her feet, steadying herself against the table. "Because blood will be spilled. So you take him, Count. I'll provide a second of my own after supper."

Chapter 13.

"No," said Alice.

"But hardly anyone here has seen you," Viola argued. "You've but to put on Basty's other coat and breeches—"

"I doubt they'd be too tight on me. Besides, even if hardly anyone has seen me, absolutely no one has seen any other such young gentleman at all and—oh, Vi, however could you be so stupid?"

Viola took a deep breath. "You don't seem to understand, Allie, that we've stumbled into something serious. Devilish serious. If he gets across the water with everything he must know by now—"

"French officers are escaping every day!" said Alice.

"That's nothing to the point—"

"Are we going to chase about everywhere challenging them all to duels? Oh, Vi, how *could* you? You might be killed—"

"Then I shall die for England!"

"And what shall we tell your family, and ... and what will become of me?"

"Keep your voice down a little," said Viola. "If I'm killed, then you'll have to go to the authorities at once and tell them everything. Denounce him for dueling if they won't believe spying. At least it'll keep him in the country."

"And why on earth didn't you simply denounce him to the whole roomful of people at once?"

"Because they probably wouldn't have believed it. The man has forged papers and a deuced persuasive presence. Besides..." Viola shrugged. "Well, it's an affair of honor. It's gone beyond just squeaking beef on him. I owe him the first round man to man."

"Oh, and then when he murders you, he ought to win the right to go on about his business scot-free."

"No!" said Viola. "That is...not for the sake of England. But..."

"So it'll all come to the same thing in the end, whether you're killed or not."

"Dash it, Alice, you don't understand the honor of the thing."

"No, and I don't understand a single thing about the code of dueling, either. So I'd make a miserable second, and I think all this going about in your brother's clothes has addled your brains."

"D'you call partiotism an addling of the brain? By God, I think I've got more in common with Count Modrowski than with you... Well, come on and we'll talk about it over supper."

"If you have so much in common with Count Modrowski," said Alice, "I think you'd best come to an understanding with him before you kill yourselves with this—this wicked nonsense. And if you can't find a second, you can't very well fight, can you? And I don't want any supper. I couldn't eat a bite, not now!"

So Viola supped alone in their private parlor, musing on the decay of patriotic fire in her generation and sex. The inn fare, though adequate to fill her stomach, could not of itself inspire her to immediate reconciliation with the friend she now perceived as a middle-class and

134

pedestrian soul who put personal convenience above the clarion calls of Country and Duty.

She rounded off her lonely meal with a bottle of port and returned to the taproom. Count Modrowski was no longer about, but his second was, and Viola requested this helpful gentleman to enlist Sir George or anyone else in the neighborhood to act for her. This was highly irregular, but there was very little regularity to any aspect of the affair, and in her practical, womanly way Viola regarded the result as more crucial than the etiquette.

"Shall we say seven A.M.?" inquired Modrowski's second.

"Six," she replied. "Well...half past six, anyhow. My sister and I have a long distance to travel tomorrow."

"Assuming this matter concludes happily, of course," he replied with a grin that seemed to have no great depth of friendly feeling.

"To a happy conclusion," she repeated, pretending to lift a glass. My honorable opponent the spy, she thought, wouldn't flash that lip-smacking sort of smile at me. Give him his due.

She called for a bottle of the Rein Deer's best brandy, took it up to her bedroom, climbed into bed without so much as knocking at Alice's door, and drank herself into a drowsiness that kept the nightmares at bay until close to dawn.

Meanwhile, August Modrowski sat in his room writing a long letter to his widowed and very independent-minded mother, who had survived all upheavals in their home country well enough to set up comfortably in Warsaw and contemplate a second marriage with one of several French and Polish officers.

It was not an easy message to compose, even though he wrote in his native language. The face of the strange

135

young Englishman came into his mind each time his pen paused on the page, and by the time he could return to the task in hand, the ink would be dry and the quill must be dipped again, or even retrimmed. He trimmed one pen away in this fashion, and since he had only two with him in his room, he saw he must either concentrate or cut his letter short.

This boy, this Mr. Williams, he was obviously such another patriot as young August Modrowski had been at about that age, with more fire than self-control. But without such a campaign as noble Kosciuszko's to fight in, and with parents or another reason to stop him from regular soldiering for some years yet. And he could not wait until all the battles he saw from the low hillock of his teenage had been fought. No, young Mr. Williams would make his own small, glorious little battles against Bonapartists.

For until Modrowski revealed himself as loyal in heart and spirit to *l'Empereur,* Mr. Williams had been comradely, warm with promise of friendship. So it was not Count Modrowski the boy fought in his thoughts, it was Bonaparte, "that monster." Modrowski had decided even before taking up the hurled gage what he himself would do tomorrow, or he would never have agreed to duel. What Mr. Williams would do seemed very sure also, considering his young passion and zealous hatred for "the Corsican butcher." Much depended upon whether Mr. Williams shot well or badly.

Yet it was not this thought that most disturbed the Polander. What preyed at him worse than foolish death was that this Caesar Williams, this young English esquire and gentleman, had struck him from first glimpse as incomparably more beautiful than any Englishwoman he had seen. Shaken to the roots of his Catholic soul, Modrowski was searching his conscience for memories of any Polish or even French lady who had affected

136

him in his own green years as this boy did now; and that he had never been so affected by any young comrade through all his army life was little comfort... when taps sounded on his bedroom door.

"Entrez," he said, correcting it at once to "Come in." He braced himself for another visit from this unpleasant *témoin,* returning with some new instructions about time and weapons as his excuse to draw pleasure from other men's fears.

But it was not his second. It was a pretty young girl with yellow curls. By her nice muslin gown and cashmere shawl, she could not be a chambermaid; by the tiny little cap on her head she ought to be a mature lady, but even in rushlight her face said to him that she should have a duenna, not be one.

He stood quickly, while she hesitated in the doorway. "Ma'am," he said, "I think you make a mistake."

"Count M—Modrowski?"

"Yes, I am he. But—"

"Oh, finally! I did make several mistakes, sir, and it was very embarrassing, but at last I found the bootcatcher and he directed me.... Am I speaking too fast?"

"You speak fast, but very clear, ma'am." The doubt crossed his mind that perhaps she was a courtesan come to the duelist on the possible eve of his death, and if so it might be good to buy her comfort and forget young Mr. Williams.

"Had I best... Perhaps I'd best come in?" she suggested. "It's very drafty and open, standing here in the passage like this."

If she was a courtesan, she must be a very new one, or very clever. He decided to behave on the assumption she was respectable. "I think you are not wise to come into my room alone, ma'am. You cannot find your own, is this so?"

"Oh, I... Yes, I think I can find my own, but... Well,

you see, your lordship, I... Mr. Williams is... He's my brother."

"Ah! This explains much."

"And I've come to you, you see, because there's no reasoning with him tonight, and it's all so very foolish!"

Modrowski nodded. "It's very, very foolish, ma'am. I agree. But do not worry for your dear brother."

She glanced around. "May I come in, sir? Someone might see me, and even though nobody knows me hereabouts..."

He spread his hands. "Very well. As you wish, good lady. I will not hurt you." To his mixed emotions, he found she offered him not the least temptation to take advantage of her obviously innocent desperation, that he was much relieved she was not a courtesan. And yet she was surely very pretty, very winsome.

She came in, glanced around again, and closed the door. The slight wind of its closing fluttered her tiny cap. He saw it was folded from a handkerchief. She put up her small, plump hand to hold it down.

"Do not worry for your brother," he repeated.

"Then you'll.... You don't mean to go through with this beastly duel?"

"Beastly. This means, 'like the beast,' does it not? But when two beasts fight... two of the same kind, same species," he said slowly, remembering boyhood glimpses, "two stags in a forest, two rams in pasture, two birds... they do not kill each other, ma'am. They run together and then after it is done they both go their ways."

"But this—this isn't like that. It's more like a vile cockfight, isn't it?"

He smiled. "I would say it is more like a—how do you say—bear-baiting. But even in the cockfights, ma'am, both the cocks very often live. And in duels also."

"And sometimes they don't! Besides, cocks don't have pistols to shoot off at one another."

"But pistols have cocks, *n'est-ce pas?*"

"Pistols...cocks? Oh, you're as bad as Vi—as Caesar is! Worse, for at least he takes it seriously, he don't make bad puns about it."

"I beg your pardon humbly. I make this bad pun to learn your language with. You call your brother 'Vi'?"

She looked embarrassed. "Sometimes—for 'Victor,' you see."

"I see. And I do not think you will need to change this name tomorrow."

"You plan to...I was hoping you might refuse to fight him at all," said Mr. Williams's sister.

"I tried very hard to refuse, ma'am. To try harder would be very rude."

"Oh. And I suppose it would be very rude simply not to appear on the field tomorrow?"

"Worse than rude." He sighed. "This would be dishonorable."

"Your lordship," she said softly, "my brother means to kill you if...if he can. And I believe he is rather a good shot, if the range is close enough."

"I did not think he wanted this duel to make noise only. But perhaps the range will not be close enough, eh?" He tried to cheer her with a smile and a wink.

She was not cheered. "He thinks—oh, it's too ridiculous—you see, he thinks you're a spy for Bonaparte!"

"He thinks this?"

She was breathing hard, as if not quite convinced herself that it might not be so. "He thinks you are on your way out of the country with all sorts of military secrets, and if he doesn't stop you, no one else will and...and Bonaparte may overrun the world!"

"But if I am a spy and have these secrets, I do not travel to Bluebriar near Haltwhistle in Northumberland. I hurry to south coast and across *la Manche*—the Channel. I think it would not be bad thing if *l'Empereur* rules the world, but I do not serve him any more. I have given my parole."

"You have? We—Caesar was sure you had not."

Modrowski smiled. "Your brother is a very great patriot. He hates all Bonapartists as we Polish hate Russians and Prussians and Austrians. But I am a good country gentleman now, and I stay in England."

"I'm so glad!... Only I wish you wouldn't stay here in Doncaster tonight, or...or...God knows whether or not we can persuade Vi you don't mean to sell us all to the French."

He bowed and came close enough to kiss her hand. "I stay in England with honor, even if this means I stay deep in the ground of England. But I think this will not happen. I have fought in great battles and lived. I think we will stand far apart tomorrow, dear ma'am, and we will both live, your dear brother and I. Now perhaps you must go, or your brother challenges me a second time for your dear sake, will he not?"

"Yes, you're right, I oughtn't stay any longer. Oh, dear! I hope you don't think..."

"I think you are a very good lady who loves her brother very much."

"And I think you are a very brave gentleman, sir, and—and you shall *not* die tomorrow, not if there's anything I can do to stop it!"

"I shall sleep easy tonight for your words. Your very humble servant, ma'am." He kissed her hand again and escorted her out, making sure the passage was clear before he saw her through the door.

It did not occur to him until afterwards to wonder why Mr. Williams had assumed he was breaking his parole. But he found a ready answer in Mr. Williams's zeal that believed nothing good of Bonapartists.

* * *

Alice did not remember until after reaching her room in safety that she had also meant to tell the count of their meeting with his friend Mr. Standeven.

This was a minor point, however, beside her doubt whether she ought not to have revealed Viola's sex. Surely that must have stopped all possibility of the morrow's duel. But she could picture her friend angrily denying it, and of course the method of proof was absolutely unthinkable. Moreover, to proclaim to the world that they were two young maidens traveling without a chaperon... No, it did not bear contemplation.

The count had reassured her that Vi would be quite safe, and she believed him. After all, he was Mr. Standeven's friend, and Mr. Standeven could not have been so greatly deceived in another gentleman, no matter what Vi said. Several times Alice was on the point of going to Viola at once, repeating her whole conversation with Count Modrowski and making her friend see reason. But Viola might begin to rage and storm, and that would be much too loud in the middle of the night. The whole business was so muddled already that any horrible scene seemed possible.

So Alice paced up and down her inn room, bumping into things, and resting from time to time on the bed, until at last she lay back, still fully dressed, and fell into the sleep of pure exhaustion.

Chapter 14.

Mrs. Beale had proposed, and Lord Spottiswood seconded the motion, that they proceed from the Red Lion Inn to Markham House near Wigan in the hope their quarry had been bound thither when Mr. Standeven encountered them in Leek. Remembering that Miss Markham—if it was indeed she—and her companion had learned from him of the captain's early return, Standeven thought it unlikely they would have gone to Markham House, but he was outvoted. Sir Toby clutched at the straw of hope, while Duncton and Miss Merriweather were enthusiastic about the detour and the chance to sleep in a private house that night.

Of course, they did not find the elopers there, nor had the captain yet come home. It was decided that Mr. Standeven should take advantage of the long summer daylight and return to Liverpool that same evening, after some necessary refreshment, to find Alice's father. The others would spend the night here and continue north next morning, whether or not Mr. Standeven had rejoined them with the captain. They could all plan to meet in Longtown, hard by the Scottish border.

As the six of them waited in the drawing room for the servants to put together a substantial tea, Miss

Merriweather asked Mrs. Beale, with a hint of malice, "And what'll you say to Captain Markham when he finds how you've let his daughter flit, eh, ma'am?"

"That my chief mistake lay in countenancing her acquaintance with your charge," Mrs. Beale replied quietly. "Sir Toby, do try to restrain yourself. Too much excess of emotion is not good for the health."

"Aye," said the old knight. "Aye, it's all your fault, ma'am! Bless us, what do I know about little gals and their ways? I trusted you, ma'am!"

"Thus you may put all the blame upon my shoulders and so exonerate yourself with your son," Mrs. Beale concurred. "If he should elect to play the melodramatic father and cast his child out for her alleged disgrace, she will always find a comfortable home with me."

Merriweather having failed again in her attempts to flutter Mrs. Beale, Noddy Duncton decided to play a desperate trump card on his friend Spotty. "And Viola will find her refuge with me," he offered, looking at Spottiswood. "Only fair, seeing it was me and Miss Merriweather set 'em to this caper."

Spottiswood raised one eyebrow. "Interesting," he said.

"What?" cried Standeven, who was standing by the fireplace.

Sir Toby jumped to his feet and made inarticulate noises.

"Sit down and take deep breaths," Mrs. Beale advised him. "I'll pour you some brandy."

"You've—you've put the young lady up to ruining herself?" Standeven went on, taking a few steps toward Duncton. "By God, I'll call you out!"

"I think not." Still seated, Lord Spottiswood crossed one leg over the other. "In fact, the matter grows more ludicrous than serious with this revelation. Not that I had not suspected it."

"You'll have t' wait your turn, sir!" Sir Toby stammered at Standeven. "Me and my son Robert first, and then you can take him on if there's anything left!"

Mrs. Beale gave the old knight a glass of brandy. "I think, Mr. Duncton," she remarked, "you had better explain yourself more fully before these gentlemen allow emotion to conquer reason. You confirm, then, that Miss Markham's pretended seducer is Lord Spottiswood's ward in masculine disguise?"

"Aye, blundertongue," said Miss Merriweather, giving Duncton a glance in which disgust at his precipitance mingled clearly with pride at Spottiswood's continued calm. "May as well tell 'em everything, now you've begun."

Duncton sighed. "Well, it wasn't entirely our notion, at that. Viola hatched it. We just thought it was a pleasant little contrivance and went along. So rest easy, sir, it's only Miss Ayrsford with your granddaughter, got up in her brother's clothes, and no man with 'em."

Sir Toby did not appear much comforted. Instead of resting easy, he choked on his brandy.

Mrs. Beale slapped his back, meanwhile inquiring, "And their true destination, Mr. Duncton?"

"Longtown," he confessed. "They'll be waiting for us at the Graham Arms, if we haven't caught 'em up before then."

"Convenient," said Lord Spottiswood.

"But what—why— The devil with it!" exclaimed Standeven. "They're risking their reputations on a—on a schoolboy hoax that ain't even worthy of a woman's mind?"

"Here!" snapped Miss Merriweather. "The female mind's every bit the equal o' the male, young man!"

The corners of Mrs. Beale's mouth twitched slightly. So, Duncton thought, did one corner of Spottiswood's as the two exchanged a glance.

"Yes, your lordship," said Mrs. Beale, "I can believe it well enough of your cousin Miss Ayrsford, but it seems less characteristic of Sir Toby's granddaughter."

"Having given the matter some thought," Spottiswood replied, "I form the theory that not even Viola would do this for the mere sport. Hence, we may hypothesize there is some additional motive involved, say, lucre. Well, Duncton? Have I conjectured aright? How much hangs upon the outcome of this adventure?"

"Five thousand yellow boys and fourteen shillings," said Duncton. "Twenty-five hundred apiece put up by Merriweather and me at even odds."

"And seven shillings apiece staked by the young ladies," said Mrs. Beale. "At least Alice shows her prudence in that."

"And what, if I may ask it," said Spottiswood, "are the exact terms of the wager? A simple race to Longtown?"

Before Duncton could add the final revelation, Miss Merriweather closed the subject with all the authority of her advanced age. "No, no, Cousin Launcelot, we've told you enough for one night. We ain't called off our wager yet, and there's still the chance one or other on us will win it."

"Fascinating." Lord Spottiswood recrossed his legs. "Well, Mr. Standeven, I think you may now enjoy a night's sleep and return to Liverpool in the morning."

Standeven clenched and unclenched his fist. "With your lordship's good grace or without it, I'll still ride tonight. They're two young ladies traveling without a protector."

"I think you undervalue them," said Spottiswood. "But have your way."

"We shall leave a letter for Captain Markham with his housekeeper," Mrs. Beale added, "in case you miss him in Liverpool."

"The thought occurs to me," said Spottiswood, "that Viola's brother, being in the Lake District for his vacation, might also have the right to know of this. A letter to Lowood Inn should stand a chance of reaching his hand soon enough to enable him to join us in Longtown."

Chapter 15.

True to last night's instructions, the bootcatcher at the Rein Deer roused Viola at six by banging on her door and calling through the keyhole until she answered. Her head throbbed, but she tried to ignore it. She dressed, opened the door, put on her polished boots, and drank the now tepid coffee the servant had left for her in the passage. Another glance at the clock showed her that all this had required twenty minutes. She was glad she had not asked to be woke any earlier, for the less time she had for preparation, the fewer thoughts she could rethink.

She rapped softly at Alice's door and got no reply. She put her ear to the keyhole and heard a very gentle snoring. It seemed a good omen. For once, Alice was still fast asleep, so she need not be bullied into keeping to her room until all was over.

Viola considered making a last use of the chamber, but she could not risk being late on the field of honor, for that—if the seconds were conscientious—might result in a cancellation of the whole business. If they were not conscientious, they might simply put back the hands of their watches until she arrived, but with the fate of Britain and her allies hanging upon the spy's death, Viola felt she could not take unjustified chances.

She hurried downstairs and found a short gentleman in the lobby. "Williams?" he said on seeing her. "Evans, sir, friend of a friend and your friend for the meeting. Your servant. Brandy? Glass of wine?"

She shook his hand and her head. "Best get to the field, Mr. Evans."

"Sure? You could drink it on the way. Besides, the field's not four minutes' walk."

"I shall not lose my steadiness in a few minutes' wait after we arrive, Mr. Evans."

He consulted his watch. "Well, you're probably right. Better early than late. Don't mind telling you, though, Williams," he added as they set out, "I'd have chose a place farther removed from the buildings."

"Nonsense. Everyone connected with the Rein Deer must know about it anyhow. Besides, my sister and I want to make an early start as soon as the business is done." Though this was not untrue, Viola's chief reason for having desired a site within easy walk of the inn was that if she failed, plenty of people would be nearby to prevent Modrowski's escape.

"Much better style to arrive in carriages," said Evans.

"At the moment, sir, I prefer convenience to style. Else what is the use of being in the country?" said Viola in her best Town superiority.

Evans shrugged.

Viola remembered that with Alice absent, no one else would know the Polander was a spy. She ought to confide in Evans, so that if Modrowski shot her through the heart, they would not in their ignorance permit him to walk away. But she reflected that if he did shoot her through the heart, the surgeon would almost certainly discover her sex on the spot when he examined

148

the wound, and that would cause enough hubble-bubble to keep everyone at hand until Alice arrived.

They reached the field. Not until she saw him waiting did Viola realize that Modrowski might have made good his escape last night. She dismissed the thought at once, in scorn.

Modrowski stood nearest the path, apart from his second and the surgeon, who were measuring off the field. As Viola came up, he stepped into her path.

"Here," said Evans. "Tell your second and let him pass it to me. Not that it ain't a bit late now."

The count glanced at Evans as at a bit of cork in the wine, then handed Viola a folded and sealed paper. "Mr. Williams, you are the only person here whom I trust with this."

She started to slip her finger beneath the blob of wax.

He held her hand. "No. Not yet, sir. If I die. Or else you give it back to me, eh?"

Recovering from her surprise, she thrust the missive into her pocket. "If this is some Polish custom, sir, I have nothing to give you in exchange. Unless—here, take my handkerchief."

It was her brother's handkerchief, of course, though for a moment she almost wished it were one of her own. The count accepted it, smiled at her, patted his forehead with it, put it into his breast pocket, and went to his end of the field. Viola suffered a glimpse of war as a monstrous, hateful, wicked necessity, not glorious at all, and Cousin Launcelot was right to scorn all the poets who praised it. Must she really aim to kill? Would it not be enough to wound? No, unfortunately, it would not be enough, for he would return to his purpose as soon as he was healed.

Meanwhile, Evans joined the other second, that helpful stranger from last night, and they measured off the distance again, nodding their heads and buzzing together like huge gnats. As challenger, Viola had chosen her distance at ten yards. It seemed to take the seconds an inordinate time to fix that simple length. The surgeon found his place well out of the line of fire. The seconds wrangled about when, exactly, the pistols should be loaded, eventually decided to do it after the selection, and took the borrowed sandalwood case to Modrowski to give him first choice. He weighed both pistols, kept the second, and gave it to his man for loading. Evans watched the process, then brought Viola the remaining gun and loaded it while she looked on.

"At the count of three," Evans told her as if it were confidential, "you'll fire at will."

Five more minutes went by while the seconds positioned their principals exactly and took their own places beside the surgeon. They reminded Viola of carrion crows, and she wondered how far she could trust them to play their parts as patriotic Englishmen if she fell and the three of them had to stand alone against Modrowski.

When all were in place, Evans repeated for everyone's benefit: "At count of three, gentlemen, raise your weapons and fire at will."

The other second uttered the numbers: "One... two... three!"

Viola lifted her pistol and began taking careful aim.

Modrowski lifted his, swung it to the right, and deliberately fired into a distant stretch of unoccupied grass.

Viola's arm jerked back. "You—you've deloped!" she screamed at her opponent.

"Deloped?" he repeated. At ten paces she could see the breadth of his smile very clearly. "Yes. I have deloped."

"Sir, damme!" She struggled to keep her voice steady

and low-pitched. "It's against the Code to take the field for nothing but mere silly children's play!"

"I do not want this fight," he replied, still smiling. "I never want to take the field today."

She bit her lip and blinked back tears of outrage. "Well, it won't save you, sir! Damme, *I* didn't come here for children's play." She took aim again, this time steadying her right hand on her left arm. He just stood there, calmly presenting her his full front. Her ball would pass through his breast pocket and the handkerchief she had given him a few minutes ago, on its way into his heart.... She couldn't help that. She blinked again and started to squeeze the trigger.

"Viola!"

Alice burst upon the scene. At her cry, Viola's shot went wide.

Viola spun and shouted. "Dash it, Alice, what the devil—"

"Just thank goodness I got here in time! Oh, you great idiot!"

The others were closing in. Modrowski reached them first. "Viola?" he said. "This is woman's name, *pravda?*"

"I have a sister of that name, sir," said Viola, amazing herself with her quick thinking under impossible circumstances. "We look rather alike. This—this teasing wench knows the surest way to fluster me is to call me by my sister's name."

With that, she thrust the empty pistol into Evans's hand, turned, and strode away from them back to the inn.

She gained last night's private parlor without having to brush past too many staring servants and bystanders, and shut herself in. Neither breakfast nor coffee awaited. Pistols for two, coffee for one... it must be set out elsewhere, probably in the taproom where everything had started. She didn't care. She was nei-

151

ther hungry nor thirsty—except perhaps for the liquor Mr. Evans had tried to press on her not half an hour ago.

She sat, pulled out Modrowski's paper, broke it open and unfolded it, expecting to find some confirmation of his espionage, even the actual military secrets.

It was a codicil to his last will and testament, dated yesterday, witnessed, apparently, by two of the inn people, and leaving the estate of Bluebriar in Northumberland, with all its rents and income, to Mr. Caesar and Miss Williams, with the sole provision that the testator be buried somewhere in this property.

She was about to crumple the paper, put her head down on the table, and sob, when someone rapped on the door. "Caesar?" It was Alice's voice.

"Come in, then!" Viola called it out in a gruff tone to hide her weepiness.

Alice came in, followed by Count Modrowski. Viola stood and whipped the codicil toward him. "Here. Yes, I opened it. Call me out if you like."

He took it, refolded it, put it back in his pocket. "You see, I am not a spy, Mr. Williams. You may search my clothes, my room, my portmanteau."

She shook her head and sat down again. "I feel a fool. I feel fool enough already. I feel the greatest fool in the world."

He simultaneously won her gratitude and heaped more coals on her head by neither agreeing nor disagreeing. "But all is well which ends well, true? Now you will take breakfast with me."

She released a long, ragged sigh. "Sir, we should be honored."

"But one point," he said as they three sat over their kippers and ham. "You spoke on the field of Miss Viola, your sister. You have two sisters?"

152

Viola coughed and tried to exchange a glance with Alice.

Alice engrossed herself in spreading marmalade on a piece of toast. "Yes, brother," she said, "and you also called me a 'teasing wench,' you know."

"Did I? Well, you deserved it."

"And your other sister, this Miss Viola," Modrowski went on. "The one who looks rather alike you. She is at home? She is an old, married sister? Or she is young and...the word? Heart-free?"

Viola coughed again, swallowed some coffee, and thought how absurdly Shakespearian it all was. "Well, Count, I suppose we'd better make a clean breast before you ferret it out anyhow."

"Ferret," he repeated.

"Strict confidence, of course. Gentleman to gentleman."

"My hand on it, sir," he replied. "And ma'am."

Alice stared up heedless of the marmalade dripping from her toast over her fingers to the plate.

"Well, sir," Viola continued, "as you're in a fair way of nosing it out, here's our secret. We ain't really brother and sister, y' see. Alice...Miss Monro here...she does me the honor to return my love, and we're on our way to Gretna Green to be married."

Modrowski let his knife and fork fall with a clatter. Alice quickly took a bite of toast.

"This is not..." Modrowski began. "I hear of this Gretna Green. It is not entirely...*comme il faut?*"

"Wicked parents," said Alice, swallowing with a visible effort

"Exactly!" Viola agreed at once, though she would have preferred to find some more original fabrication. "Wicked parents, hers and mine, all four. Leave us no other course."

Now that he had had a moment to digest the idea,

Modrowski's predominant emotion seemed to be relief, even enthusiasm. Unfortunately, his next words did nothing to awaken similar emotions in Viola's breast. "Ah—wicked parents!" he cried. "Yes, I see. Then I come with you to Gretna Green, hey? I am your friend— your escort, your brideman. And then after, if you need place to live, there is Bluebriar, *n'est-ce*—is it not so?"

Chapter 16.

"We...er...we've cost you enough time and expense already, sir," said Viola.

"It is nothing." Count Modrowski smiled like a man recognizing his true role in the history of the universe.

She tried again. "But Bluebriar is calling you, *n'est-ce pas?*"

"It will wait."

"You're exceedingly kind, sir," Alice murmured, "but might it not be best for you to make sure Bluebriar is prepared to receive guests?"

"You are the most important, dear ma'am. It is no use to prepare the house and no guests come."

"Dash it, sir," exclaimed Viola, "you're not suggesting I ain't man enough to take care of Miss—er—Monro by myself?"

Modrowski spread his hands. "No more dueling, dear sir. From wolves and brigands, yes, you protect her very well. But your wicked parents search for two, not so? If they hear of three who travel together, they suspect nothing. We drag dead cat across the trail."

Unable to shake his purpose, the young women withdrew after breakfast on the pretext of needing more time to pack, while the count happily went down to arrange for horses and carriage.

"Well, then," said Viola, once in the privacy of her friend's room, "you'll have to take suddenly sick."

"Why should I always be the one to take sick?"

"I haven't asked it of you before. It was your own idea at the Double-Necked Swan yesterday."

"Yes, well, in a way that was my fault," Alice confessed. "It was my father Mr. Standeven turned out to know. But this time it is entirely your doing, and I think it's only fair you should be the one to take ill."

"But how the devil would it look? After being fit enough to fight a duel this morning."

"Why not simply tell him you're a woman?"

"Why not...why not?" Viola's mind stumbled over conflicting emotions. "Why...why, because if we did that, there'd be no chance at all of losing him. He'd insist on seeing us safe somewhere."

"Oh. And it'll be so much better if he sees us safely wed to each other in Gretna Green. What on earth should we do then?"

"Don't be silly. It couldn't be binding."

"How do we know it couldn't? Viola, I absolutely refuse to be married to another woman, and if—if..." Alice's gray eyes seemed about to brim over.

"Oh, very well." For all her assured front, Viola was not quite sure what embarrassment and red tape might ensue from such a contract. "We'll tell him when we get to Gretna and there's no other help for it."

"And then, being the gentleman he is, he will insist upon marrying one of us rather than having compromised us both."

"You've read too many romantic novels."

"*I've* read too many romantic novels! Whose notion was this whole extravagant masquerade?"

Viola sighed and drummed her fingertips on her

cheek. "I don't see anything else for it. I'll have to write to Sebastian. He's only a county and a half away. If I write at once, the letter should reach him tonight or tomorrow morning. Then he and his friend can meet us this side of the Border, pretend to be your brothers, and rescue you from me. If we haven't been able to give Count Modrowski the slip before then."

"Yes," said Alice a little dryly. "That should answer very well. I wish I had never agreed to come with you on this—this scatterbrained enterprise!"

"Well, *I* don't," Viola replied. "I'm very glad we came. I have found it an...an education. And you must stay sick in bed today, so that Basty will have time to reach the Border before us. Only one day, I swear," she added as her friend still looked rebellious. "By tomorrow, I'll have thought of something else to stall our trip."

Mr. Sebastian Ayrsford had been enjoying a restful vacation, tramping about the Lake District in the day, reading poetry and travel books in the evening, and hearing no one's pleasantries except his school chum Hector Hobart's, only a comparatively small proportion of which were really annoying. If that proportion had seemed to be on the increase of late, no doubt it was because Hector was less attuned to rustication, less content to find his chief excitement in mereside rambles and nightly chess games.

So although the letter they found waiting at Lowood Inn on their latish return that fine evening was directed to Sebastian, Hector was the one who looked at it with the more enthusiasm. "Here it is, old fellow. So someone does care about us in our self-imposed exile. Even if it's only someone who writes on plain paper, no scent, a man's writing or I miss my bet."

"It appears to be Lord Spottiswood's hand," said Sebastian.

"Even if it's only your guardian. Writing to let us know he's bought his commission and it's off to the wars at last."

Sebastian tapped the letter on his hand. "You know his lordship might as well be a Quaker for all the likelihood there is of his ever joining the army."

"Well, open it, old man. Maybe he's offering us a pair of colors, too."

"Confound it, Hector, I wish you wouldn't joke at a time like this. It's probably bad news, or why would he be writing?"

"No black edge to it, is there? But come on, Basty, see what he has to tell you," Hector went on a little more gently. "Better than stewing things up in your own imagination."

Sebastian broke the wafer, unfolded the epistle, and read it through. For a moment his friend wondered uneasily just how bad the news could be. Then Sebastian found relief in some of the strongest expressions his rather austere vocabulary included. "Damn and blast the devil!" he ended superfluously. "Well, you'll have to learn a good lot of it in any case, you might as well know it all at once." He passed the note over for his friend's edification.

It was dated the day before, from a place called Markham house, near Wigan, Lancashire, and read:

"Sir,
Duncton, Cousin Merriweather, and your sister have entered upon a wager. The exact terms remain mysterious, but at the present moment Viola appears to be journeying northward with a single companion of about her own age, one Miss Markham (not yet of your acquaintance), in a pretended elopement to Gretna Green. Their co-conspirators

158

inform us the true destination is Longtown, where we will hope you have opportunity to meet us at the Graham Arms. If you should glimpse the young ladies on your way, the knowledge that Viola left London disguised in garments appropriated from your wardrobe may help you to recognize her even at a distance.

Yours, &c.,
Spottiswood.

Hector whistled, then laughed. "Lord, Basty, but that sister of yours is a rare one!"

"Like to be raw in certain tender areas by the time we're done blistering her for this last prank." Sebastian set his teeth.

Hector laughed again. "Ten pounds to a shilling she ain't! Only wish I'd known the old birch as little as she."

"Well, she is very likely to make its acquaintance before the week's out this time." In the effort of quelling his emotion, Sebastian struck his own thigh. "We may as well cry quits to our vacation."

"What, not sorry, are you? Sounds like a rum outing to me."

Sebastian glared at him. "I rejoice that you find something to look forward to with pleasure."

"The bad news could have been death or dismemberment, you know," Hector replied cheerily. "House burned to the ground, fortune lost in shipwreck, favorite foxhound dead of chilblains—"

"I'll start packing," said Sebastian. "You can arrange for a couple of good horses."

Hector yawned. "Not tonight, old fellow. Much as I look forward to these next few days, I'm not diving straight into 'em without my dinner and a good night's sleep."

In the morning a second letter awaited Sebastian, brought by the night mail coach. This time, recognizing his sister's hand, he tore it open with no need for Hector's urging. It was dated yesterday, from Doncaster, and read:

Dear Sebastian,
We are in something of a Pickle. My dear new chum Miss Markham and I were driving about on a little jaunt round the North Country—I'll tell you more details when I see you, but it's all rather Involved. For Propriety, I borrowed some of your clothes—I'll explain that later, too—and the Deuce is, we've met a sort of Polish *emigré,* really a very Decent fellow, but because of the language difficulty or for another reason, he's took the Bee into his head that I'm a young man and Miss M. and I are eloping to Gretna. The Muddle is that now he is determined to see us safe to the officiating Blacksmith. He's really a most Charming Gentleman, a Count and formerly a very Brave soldier, and we would not Hurt him for a Great deal. So if you and your chum Hector would Meet us before we reach the Border, pretend to be Miss M.'s brothers, and rescue her from me, we should be Infinitely in your debt, and since if things go well I'm in Good way of winning a very nice sum for either the Merriweather or dear old Noddy, we may be able to Sugar your pockets, too, and help make up for cutting your holidays a little short. We are stalling

our journey as best we can, to give you Time to be there before us, but we shall probably be approaching Longtown on the Carlisle Road within these two or three days, so you'd best Bestir Yourselves. We are calling Miss Markham 'Alice Monro,' you must be Sure to Remember That. Do *Not* offer any violence to Count Modrufski, who is entirely Innocent of anything but a Very Gentlemanly over-Solicitousness, tho' you may of course threaten me a Little, for the sake of appearances. Take Miss M. to the Graham Arms in Longtown, and I shall Rejoin you there as soon as possible, or else send you further Instructions. I know I have teazed you unconscionably in the past, Basty, but I am not Teazing you Now, so do be a Dear and come help us. My name is Caesar Williams, which may also come Handy for you to know. You and Hector must now be Messrs. Monro for a while, but you may as well retain your own Christian Names, so that we don't Tangle ourselves up addressing one another in the Press of the moment. I'm sorry it will be Impossible for you to Answer this, since we can not Risk receiving any letters under the very well-form'd nose of our Count Modruwski, but we rely wholly upon you, and if you do not come to help us near Longtown, we shall simply have to Do it All Ourselves, so if you read this and if you don't wish to see your sister married to Alice Markham, of Course you'll be there Ready to Play your Part.

Your Very Loving, grateful,
and Affectionate Sister,
V.

Sebastian crumpled the sheet into a ball and threw it in that shape to Hector, who smoothed it on the edge of the table, read it through in his turn, and laughed. "Lord, what a wench your sister is! I love her with all my heart and soul."

"I don't," said Sebastian.

"And next time I rusticate, I'll do it with her instead of you, you Friday-face."

Sebastian scowled. "We should have started last night."

"And missed this letter? Not for anything, old man! You should be eternally grateful to your sluggardy old chum Hector."

"At least it'll be something to show Lord Spottiswood. Maybe it'll help throw some light on what he already knows of the business."

"Miss Markham—Monro may help explain things, too, when we bring her in with us." Hector continued to smooth creases from the sheet while rereading it. "I wonder if she'll turn out to be another nonpareil like your sister Vi? Miss Alice Monro, my own dear sister for the next few days—I love her, too, already, unknown and unseen."

"Gamon. And we'd better look up his lordship first and see what he thinks of this."

Hector shrugged. "And miss meeting the charming Miss Markham at our earliest opportunity? Well, your guardian will probably be there first anyhow. I hope the Graham Arms is prepared for us all!"

Chapter 17.

Being two healthy young men on horseback, with fewer than sixty miles to cover, Sebastian and Hector were in Longtown by evening of the same day. Being two strong and healthy older men on horseback, and having started from Liverpool before dawn the day before, Captain Markham and Mr. Standeven had arrived much earlier. With a carriage to handle and a somewhat less keen collective sense of urgency (despite Sir Toby's tantrums), Lord Spottiswood, Mrs. Beale, and their companions arrived midtime between and so were on hand to introduce Mr. Ayrsford and his friend, when they came, to the captain and lieutenant, who would not otherwise have known them.

From the outset, Alice's father was disinclined to approve of Miss Ayrsford's brother, as of all her family and old friends, and of Mrs. Beale for allowing the situation to develop. Indeed, perhaps the only people present of whom Captain Markham was inclined to approve were his own father—out of strict filial loyalty—and James Standeven.

The nine relatives and friends of the errant young ladies assembled as soon as possible in the largest private room to be had and held council before supper.

Sebastian solemnly produced Viola's note, and Lord Spottiswood read it aloud without commenting on its worse-for-wear condition.

"Modrowski!" cried Standeven the first time Spottiswood read that word.

His lordship cocked an eyebrow. "You know the name?"

"My old prisoner and chum—war breeds close friendships, sir," the lieutenant replied. "And men come to know one another well. I'll personally vouch for Modrowski's honor. Depend on it, if he's with them, they're as safe as if they were under my own protection."

"There is not likely to be more than one Polish count of that name in England at the moment," said Mrs. Beale.

Lord Spottiswood read the rest of his ward's letter without further interruption, then passed it around, beginning with Mrs. Beale.

His lordship opened the discussion by remarking, "There is a high factor of improbability in this."

"True," said Mrs. Beale. "Nevertheless, the situation exists. And I have schooled myself for any improbability since the first shock of Miss Markham's unwonted behavior."

"Aye, madam." Captain Markham clapped his fist on the table. "And she cut herself adrift while under your care and guidance. That wants some pretty explaining."

"It does indeed, sir," the widow agreed. "We will hope she can provide it."

"Aye, aye, m'lass," muttered Miss Merriweather (forgetting wager and old animosity for the moment). "Give it to him, the long-faced looby."

"But first get her back safe!" urged Sir Toby. "Only

get her back safe! Lord! Traipsing about the whole country with a foreigner!"

"I tell you, sir," Standeven repeated, "your granddaughter's honor's as safe with August Modrowski as it'd be with myself."

"Aye, mebbe, but who'll believe it?" said Miss Merriweather.

"Besides," said Hector Hobart, in reply to Sir Toby rather than Miss Merriweather, "Count What's-his-name thinks she's another man's intended—namely, Vi Ayrsford's."

Sir Toby uttered ejaculations of despair, and Miss Merriweather passed him her smelling bottle.

"I wish your ward were in fact the man she pretends to be, sir," said Captain Markham, glowering at Lord Spottiswood. "I would see that she did marry my daughter, after exposing her to this scandal."

Perhaps it was only coincidence that in concluding this speech Miss Markham's father directed a glare at Miss Ayrsford's twin brother, but that young man coughed nervously and protested, "Here, sir, I ain't even acquainted with your daughter, and I'd have whipped Viola blue if I'd known what she was planning."

Mr. Standeven turned to Captain Markham. "Sir, I am acquainted with your dear daughter, if only by chance and briefly, and I request your permission to make her my formal addresses."

The captain with a handshake, and Sir Toby with babbles of joy, bestowed their gratitude upon Standeven for saving the child from disgrace.

Meanwhile, Hector's fertile brain was conceiving. "Look'ee, it's too late to whip your sister blue beforehand, but why not teach her a roaring good lesson she'll never forget, that'll make her think some before playing us such a trick again?"

"I do not approve," said his lordship, "of whipping the human body into any unnatural color."

"Yes, sir, and this is the result!" said Sebastian rebelliously. "If she'd been at school with us—"

"Not that *you* ever got any birching to speak of, old man," said Hector. "But I wasn't about to suggest anything like that. You recall that old, derelict gamboge-colored caravan we saw in somebody's field just outside town?"

"Yes," said Duncton, "I remember catching sight of it, too."

"Well, let's see if we can't take it, get ourselves up as gypsies, waylay the girls and make believe to kidnap 'em, and put a little wholesome fear into 'em that way?"

"Bravo!" cried Miss Merriweather with a glance at Mrs. Beale. "Are you game for it, ma'am?"

"Capital," added Noddy Duncton with a similar glance at Spottiswood. "Can we persuade you, Spotty?"

Alice's grandfather gave a little squeak and began to shake his head.

Captain Markham put both fists on the table and stood.

Lord Spottiswood looked at Mrs. Beale and the corners of his mouth quirked slightly. "I believe, madam, we are being solicited to lend ourselves to a kind of outrageous and undignified mummery."

Mrs. Beale returned his look with a similar quirking at the corners of her mouth. "Dignity, sir, resides in the quiet soul, untouchable by outer freaks and frolics."

"Well, you and your crew may discipline your young miss however you please," said Captain Markham. "But not before we have my daughter back safe in the bosom of her own family. Standeven?"

"I'm with you, sir," said the lieutenant, rising, though not without a sympathetic glance at Miss Ayrsford's people.

"Mrs. Beale," the captain went on coldly, "do you come with us, or cleave to these noble new friends of yours?"

"You have given me the impression, sir, that you are not entirely satisfied with my performance as Alice's chaperone," she replied. "While hoping that in time you may countenance some further correspondence between your daughter and myself, I cannot feel that my continued services would any longer be welcome to you or necessary to her, once she is restored to the care of her grandfather and father."

"Aye, my dear," said Miss Merriweather. "Stick with us, and we'll stain you berry brown and make a right proper fortune-telling gypsy crone of you."

Mrs. Beale turned quietly toward the last speaker. "I believe, ma'am, you had best be the crone with cards and crystal. I shall content myself with a lesser role."

"Very good, ma'am," said the captain. "*Messieurs, mesdames.* By your leave." He beckoned Sir Toby to his feet and gave the company a curt nod.

"Before you leave us, Captain," Lord Spottiswood remarked, "I think you'd be well advised to help us calculate how long we may have to prepare for the young ladies' arrival and precisely how and at what point you will extract Miss Markham before the rest of us descend upon Miss Ayrsford in our gypsy disguise."

Chapter 18.

The morning after Alice's pretended indisposition at Doncaster, the two young ladies had got up at half past five hoping to slip away, only to find Count Modrowski already at breakfast. He was delighted to see Miss Monro in good health and ready for an early start. The morning after that, they did manage to leave him behind at Leeming, only to have him catch them up before they reached Catterick. This resulted in a very delicate scene, as they searched for ways to explain without injury to his feelings why they had tried to elude his self-appointed guardianship. All they could really do was find various rephrasings of the argument, "But we've taxed your time and purse enough already, d'ye see?" He kept countering that by running away they had caused him great anxiety and he would have searched for them all the distance to Gretna Green, so that they taxed him as much time and money one way as the other, and anyhow, it was no trouble and no expense and no better way to spend his time. At last they gave him their promise not to do it again, and traveled on with him.

"But why not have hurt his feelings?" Alice asked when the young ladies were alone in her room at the

Crown in Penrith, now only twenty-seven miles from Longtown. "I know it would be a dreadful shame, he's such a dear, but it might have got rid of him for once and all."

Viola heaved a sigh that seemed to come all the way from her toes in Sebastian's slippers.

"As we had to leave Mr. Standeven in Leek," Alice went on.

"Not the same thing at all. We didn't have to insult your Mr. Standeven, nor part with him on terms that'd make it impossible to meet him again someday in polite society."

"We can hardly meet either one of them again socially in our present disguises. Especially you. So it would not have made much difference."

Viola gave another sigh. "It'd have broke my heart to insult him again. The handsomest man I've ever met..."

"Not half so handsome as Mr. Standeven!" said Alice.

"Twice as handsome! And those huge brown eyes...It'd be like kicking a faithful hound."

"I agree it would have wrenched my heart, too—"

"Not so much as mine. I'd have had to give the blow. All you'd need do would have been sit there blushing and ladylike."

"Well..." said Alice. "At any rate, you could easily have met him someday in London in your own character, even if you had to bedevil Lord Spottiswood or Miss Merriweather to ask him to dinner especially—"

"Assuming he ever returns to London from Bluebriar."

"Well, if he doesn't, you would not have got on with him in any case. And he's much more likely to return for another London Season than I ever am."

"Well..." said Viola. "Well, I'm not going back from

my word now. We'll just have to rely on Basty and Hector."

So all they could do was redouble their heroic ruses to prolong the journey. Fortunately, Penrith offered a number of quaint and historic curiosities, in which the Polander had sufficient natural interest to curb some of his sense that they should be getting along; and Carlisle, where they dined, had a number more, so that it was nearing dusk by the time they passed through Westlinton, having contrived to take almost as many days for the comparatively short distance from Doncaster as might have sufficed a determined traveler for the entire trip from London.

Viola was driving Alice in a hired gig. Finding exactly the right carriage for hire at the right price had been the time-eating project of more than an hour. Count Modrowski rode alongside, having invested in a horse of his own purchase, a fine sorrel mare he would have called by a Polish name had her previous owner not already dubbed her Fancy.

"Will they meet us this side of Longtown or the other?" Alice murmured when the count was whistling and she was sure he would not overhear.

"I only hope the clotpolls understood my note. If they don't catch us this side, we'll put up in Longtown and hope they confront us there."

"Will he let us put up in Longtown tonight, so near the Border?"

"Don't be a pebblebrain," Viola whispered. "You've but to say you want to arrive in Gretna morning-fresh for your wedding."

"He might say it'd be safest to cross into Scotland at once."

"Look!" said Viola. "Is that—no, damnation, there's three of 'em, two too big and one too old."

"Oh!" Alice looked at the two men in a chaise-and-four and the single outrider, who seemed to be poised at the branch of a crossroad, as if watching and waiting. "Oh, Vi, don't you see who it is?"

"What? No, I— Wait, that's never Standeven!"

"And my father and grandfather— Oh, Vi!"

Viola had never seen Captain Markham, and old Sir Toby had simply been part of the background in her friendship with Alice. Even Standeven's features had faded from her memory despite their party at the Swan with Two Necks, since her memory for faces was not of the best. But she could recognize her one-night drinking companion by the empty sleeve pinned up to his coat, like Lord Nelson's.

Modrowski neither knew of nor would have needed this hint—he recognized his old friend immediately the lieutenant turned his face in their direction. "Standeven?" he cried, and hardly had the Englishman given an answering shout and started his horse forward before the Polander touched spur to Fancy's flank and cantered over the remaining yards to meet him halfway.

"Oh, dear," said Alice.

"Devil and the deep!" Viola swore softly. "Well, we're in the fire now for sure."

"Can't we turn and—"

"Not devilish handy. Look!"

While Modrowski and Standeven were meeting, Captain Markham was whipping his carriage toward that of the runaways.

The captain was more practiced in the skills of maneuvering ships than land vehicles, and Viola had to back her gig in order to avoid a tangle of wheels. "Here, sir!" she cried, determined to show a bold front to the last. "What the deuce d'ye think you're doing?"

"Alice!" thundered Captain Markham.

"Oh, Allie, Allie, Allie, little Allie!" Sir Toby supplemented.

"Here, you young hell-cat, what the devil are you doing with my daughter?" the captain continued.

"Your daughter, sir?" cried Viola for lack of a better rejoinder.

Modrowski turned back to them. "This is the wicked parents?"

"Count Modrowski, sir," said Captain Markham, "if that is who you are—"

"Aye, sir, it's my chum Modrowski," Standeven testified, as both men rode close to the carriages. "And as honorable a man as any here."

"But—" Viola tried.

"Count Modrowski," the captain went on in a very loud voice, "since my friend Standeven vouches for you, I will accept your own sincere good faith in all this. I will even thank you for your part in protecting my daughter. But I must inform you that—"

"Here, sir, what the devil are you talking about?" cried Viola. The awful thought had struck her that, knowing so much, Alice's father must know all.

"That that young hoyden passing herself off as my daughter's dandy is another female!" shouted Markham.

It seemed to Viola that for a moment all was dead silence and in the next moment all was shouting and confusion, with Count Modrowski's eyes on her for an eternity. Her first thought was to shake the reins and drive away at full speed and never stop driving—but the gig was hemmed round with Markham's chaise and Modrowski and Standeven on their horses. And besides, there was Alice....

"A female!" blustered Mr. Caesar Williams at top voice. "Sir, take your daughter back for now—I'll send my man round to you—pistols at dawn and I'll have her back—here, love..." (seizing Alice's arm and half thrusting her from the gig) "...back to the bosom of your family for now, m'dear..."

Alice stared at her and scrambled down. Viola became aware that Standeven had dismounted to help her friend from the gig, but she was still more conscious of Modrowski's gaze than of anything else. The minute Alice was safe in Standeven's arm, Vi snapped the whip and swung the gig out and away. It scraped Markham's wheels in passing, and she felt a crackling sound, but she only popped her whip louder. It was fortunate she met no other traffic on the road, driving as she was like a desperate drunkard, and near blinded with dust and tears.

"Another female?" Count Modrowski was repeating. "No—this is young man. He fights duel with me...."

"We have seen her letter, sir," said Captain Markham. "Alice! This *was* the same young person with whom you left London?"

"Yes, sir," Alice confessed, clinging to Mr. Standeven.

"This spoiled, scandal-courting, hellfire young scion of the dissolute nobility—"

"Oh, please, Father, you mustn't be too hard on her!" Alice pleaded.

Still holding his beloved tight, Mr. Standeven came to the defense of her friend. "Pure high spirit, I'd guess, sir. Nothing more."

"An evil influence, Standeven. My daughter would not have done any such thing as this of her own genius."

"No, Father," said Alice, taking refuge in Mr. Standeven's smile.

"Well, let her own people see to her," Captain Markham conceded. "Though I doubt they'll only spoil her further. Alice!" he went on, as if dismissing Lord Spottiswood's ward had suddenly left him free to notice his own daughter's position. "To me at once, miss! You're not married to him yet."

"Yet?" said Alice.

Sir Toby tugged his son's arm. "But soon, Rob, soon— Aye, soon."

"If you'll have me, ma'am," Standeven murmured. "Only if you'll have me."

"Oh, yes, sir! Yes! But now perhaps I'd best..." She gave his hand a squeeze and pulled away to start the timorous but dutiful crossing to her father. Mr. Standeven accompanied her, walking at her side.

"But he denies it," said Count Modrowski. "Mr. Williams, he says he is not another young lady."

Alice paused in the act of being handed up by Mr. Standeven into her father's chaise. "Oh, Count, I'm so very sorry for deceiving you all this time," she said, looking back at him, "but she—Mr. Williams—she *is* another female—Miss Ayrsford, you see."

"Then you are not... He—she—is not...but this Gretna Green?"

"We never really meant to reach there. You see, it was all a very foolish joke, from the very beginning."

"That's right, that's right, chick," said Sir Toby, pulling her up to the seat. "That's all right now, little Allie."

"But our duel?" said the count. "This was joke, also?"

"No, she really did think you were a...a spy, Count. For a little while, only for—"

"A spy?" said Mr. Standeven. "Auggie Modrowski? What kind of nonsense—"

"And she—she is *panna*—young lady?" The count gave a great shout and spurred his horse into a gallop after the vanished gig.

"Damme!" said Captain Markham, staring after him. "You may vouch for his honor, Standeven. Can you vouch for his reason as well?"

174

"Polish," Mr. Standeven said simply. "The Poles are a passionate people."

"Aye." Alice's father lifted the reins. "Aye, and he has some right to be angry."

"I think...I don't think he was...I think he sounded rather joyful," Alice murmured, mostly to herself.

Modrowski reached Longtown without finding Miss Ayrsford on the way. It was not a great metropolis, and when he had hurried round from the Graham Arms to the stables to the Roman ruins to the few other places that would seem to offer refuge to a stranger of either sex, his eagerness turned to fear. Pausing scarcely long enough to catch his breath, he drew out the handkerchief she had given him just before their duel. She had never demanded it back and so he had kept it, although with secret tuggings of guilt and shame. The shame was now dissolved. He pressed the cloth to his lips, replaced it tenderly in his breast pocket, and spurred back along the road to Westlinton, keeping a sharp watch to all sides in the gathering dark.

Chapter 19.

As the first shock began to pass, Viola had become aware of a sinister sound in the wheel that had scraped Captain Markham's chaise. She turned into the first byroad, and almost immediately—as it seemed—the wheel came off.

Bringing the horse to a stand without injury to him or herself took her mind from even Count Modrowski for a few moments. When they were safe, she clambered down out of the wreck, finished calming the horse, and looked things over.

She had got far enough along the byroad that the gig might escape notice, if anyone going past on the highway failed to look round at the right moment. Her best plan would be to take the horse and ride bareback to...could she circle round cross-country and get back to Carlisle tonight, to disappear amongst its more than ten thousand citizens?

Reaction set in and she kicked the gig furiously with a trembling foot. "Damned carriages! This whole journey has been cursed with devil-weak wheels!" she exclaimed, thinking of the broken wheel of her own cabriolet on the first morning of the adventure and wondering dismally if she would ever drive that sweet little cab again.

At least her things were still packed in the saddle-bags purchased at Leicester. She started digging them from the skewed gig, blessing the long summer twilight in that it should enable her to consult *Kearsley's Guide* for a while yet; and cursing it, in that for a while yet it would keep darkness from concealing the evidence of her trail.

"That be fine 'orseflesh, me lord," drawled a voice behind her. At first she thought it was Hector Hobart, stretching out his syllables to a ridiculous length. But when she turned with his name on her lips, ready to give him a prime scold for letting Captain Markham intercept them sooner, she saw two gypsy-like figures in ragged garments, faded and dirtied to a dreary brown. Their skins were much the color of their clothes, their appearance relieved only by the bright bandannas around their necks and hair, and the glint of gold earrings in their ears.

"Oh," she said. "Well, fellows, if you'll lend me a hand here, there's a crown in it for each of you."

The smaller one sidled up to the horse, stroked its neck, and said in the voice she had mistook for Hector's, "Us'll give 'ee four hands now, me lord, and have considerable more siller than your two crowns for each on 'em."

"A crown apiece is very generous for a few minutes' work," she replied, deepening her voice as gruff as it would go, for she began to be uneasy. "But I'll make it a crown and a half, though it's highway robbery."

He gave a laugh that was more cackle than chuckle. "Aye, me lord, and more'n robbery, and more'n four hands to share in it, so us 'opes yer purse be as fine as yer 'orse 'ere."

"Don't talk nonsense, fellow!" Realizing that while
177

the shorter one was holding her attention she had left the taller one out of sight at her back, she tried to turn—but too late. He had come up behind her so softly she hadn't heard him, and now he clamped one hand over her mouth and the other arm around her chest and shoulders.

She managed to bite—not much or hard because his fingers were so strong, but she did catch a little flesh. He neither flinched nor cried out, but only drew in his breath and took a still firmer grip on her face from cheekbones to jaw. She kicked, and he lifted her feet from the ground, laid her flat on the road, and held her while his accomplice bound her ankles and wrists. All this, however, gave her time to digest the impression that the taller one, at least, for all his strength, seemed careful not to bruise her.

She tried to study his face, and though it was darkened, dirt-smudged, and in shadow, she was sure she recognized it. When he took his hand from her mouth, she said, "Coz Launcelot? Who docked your eyebrows?"

He shrugged, took off his neckerchief, and gagged her with it.

Then he picked her up and started carrying her through gates, over fields and furze, his companion following with the horse. But since he carried her in his arms, rather than slung across his shoulder or the horse's back, she felt more and more sure these men were her guardian and Hector. Lord Spottiswood got up as a dirty gypsy! Who would have thought it? Had Noddy or Miss Merriweather won the bet, and everyone joined in this new charade to celebrate? She was enchanted with the game. It almost took her thoughts from Count Modrowski for the time being. She decided to pretend she didn't recognize them, after all, and give them a rare mixty-maxty when the chance came.

They did not need to go very far before reaching a

178

dirty caravan with some fresh-looking cabalistic symbols daubed over its old, peeling, yellowish paint. It was camped by a stream, where a couple of bony nags pulled at the vegetation and three more gypsies, two men and a woman, were feeding a small fire and cutting food into a kettle, while an aged crone looked on from the seat of the caravan, rubbing the fringes of her red shawl over and over in her hands.

Viola guessed them to be Noddy, Basty, Miss Merriweather, and the younger woman must be Mrs. Beale! She almost giggled to see Alice's redoubtable duenna in ragged skirt and dirty face, and her own Merriweather in so convincing a mummery of crabbèd age.

The crone cackled loudly at their arrival. "Aie, aie, a lovely bit o' horseflesh ye have there, Rinalf me lad. Fetch 'n here, fetch 'n here."

Hector-Rinalf fetched it to the side of the caravan seat and the old woman ran her left hand over its neck and withers, clucking in appreciation. "Aie, a lovely, and none too soon, neither. Now one or a brace more, and we'll leave here in fine style, we will. Like these brave pale gentry, demons curse 'em." She spat.

Viola was a little shaken. She had never seen Miss Merriweather spit, for all the old dame's other free manners. But the rest of the performance was so complete that no doubt she must have practiced.

"Aie, take 'n now and rub 'n down," the old lady went on to Rinalf. Then she turned to eye Viola and her carrier. "And what have 'ee there, Gonzar? A fine gentleman for ransom, eh? Fetch 'n here, fetch 'n here."

Cousin Launcelot-Gonzar fetched Viola to the side of the caravan, where she half expected Miss Merriweather to stroke her like the horse. But the old woman only leaned close, cupping the bottom half of her own face in her brown, heavily beringed left hand. Viola was almost sure it was Miss Merriweather, but she looked very strange in this outlandish disguise.

"Aie, a troublesome 'un," drawled the crone, touching Viola for the first time—to poke her in the ribs. "A wild wolf, this 'n be. Give 'ee a fight, did he?"

Gonzar grunted, and Viola kicked at him with her bound legs to show her annoyance at the unjust accusation. So far, after the first short scuffle, she had been a model prisoner!

"These troublesome 'uns, they ben't worth the saving for ransom," the beldam went on. "Best stick a knife in atween their ribs and get 'em buried by moonlight."

Viola shook her head and made protesting noises. The joke was going a little far.

"Well, fetch 'n up in the wagon and le' me cast 'is fortune." The crone pushed herself up and ducked beneath the curtain that was drawn across the front of the caravan.

The large man did sling Viola over his shoulder now, for his own better ease in climbing up after the old woman. But once inside he arranged her comfortably enough on some soft though greasy cushions and rugs. One of the other men squeezed in after them, the one Viola could have sworn a few minutes ago must be Noddy Duncton. They squatted one on either side of her in silence while the old woman set up a small table between herself and the prisoner, lit two black candles that were already affixed in mounds of old wax to its sides, and blew out the lantern, drenching the caravan's interior with a darkness much thicker than the gloaming outside.

It was the cards that all but convinced Viola she was amongst real gypsies. She had not thought to wonder about the caravan and the bony nags. Even in this rural region, such properties should certainly be available for purchase or loan. But she had never seen cards like those the crone shuffled and laid out one by one on the table. Longer than ordinary playing cards, and much worn, they seemed to be almost entirely court cards, but the figures were drawn full length rather than double headed, so that some of them fell upside down; she did not recognize any of the suit pips; and the court cards were peopled with popes and beggars and angels as well as kings and queens. And she could see how very differently the beldam laid them out for true fortune telling than Count Modrowski had done his ordinary pack for his game of *Patience*.

(She could not know they were an incomplete pack of Tarot cards that a collector of curiosities who lived in the neighborhood, and happened to be one of the late Lord Merriweather's godchildren, had lent Miss Merriweather while Mrs. Beale was trimming the shaggy peaks from Lord Spottiswood's eyebrows; nor that Miss Merriweather had made up her pattern of snapping the cards down until the right one appeared.)

So the old gypsy turned her cards, shaking her head and muttering things like, "Trey of Rose nobles—very bad, poor ransom," and "The Moon—aie, by the light o' the moon," and "Ace of Swords, aie, the weapon itself, quick and clean," until at last she laid down a particularly gruesome card on which a skeleton with a long scythe cut at ground strewn over with severed hands and feet, and she did not need to explain that that card was Death.

"Aie, me lordling, ye'll not question the cards, as ye can see 'em spread out with yer own eyes. But look'ee here," she added, turning up her last card, which showed a man hanging upside down. "The Gallows' Bird, ye should be glad enough 't was yon Ace o' Swords came up first, else we'd ha' had to hang ye, ye silly young gaybird."

"'T would be more fun hangin' 'un," rumbled the man Viola had earlier thought was Noddy.

"Aie, so 't would, and I don't reck the how on 't makes any great difference... but nay, nay, Grumsen, the dagger's in the cards, and the quicker way's always the safer."

"Waitin' the moonlight anyhow, ain't we?" said Grumsen.

"And can dig out the grave that while, eh?" The crone gathered her cards together, tucked them into some safe corner of the caravan, blew out the candles, and herded the men outside, Grumsen still arguing that it would be more fun to hang the prisoner. The biggest gypsy, Gonzar, had never opened his mouth, which helped metamorphose him from Cousin Launcelot into the most frightening kidnapper of all. Viola wondered if he would be the one to wield the dagger, and shuddered.

A loud laugh went up outside, then a mumble of voices, then another laugh. Then they started talking about their supper, which was cooking on the small campfire. Viola tried to work her bonds loose, but every few moments one or another of her captors would look in at her with a lantern, always in silence. Despite everything, their supper smelled good whenever they lifted the caravan curtain and the air wafted in. She lay and clung to the almost completely vanished hope that they really were her family and friends after all, teaching her a lesson.

Dusk was almost complete now, without as well as within. The fire cast some wavering light and shadows through the curtain. By the sounds, Viola guessed the gypsies were settled down to their supper. That might give her a few moments.

The gag had been tied over but not in her mouth, and her hands bound in front of her. She lifted them

182

and worked the gag free, then set to work with her teeth on the rope around her wrists. It did not taste pleasant, and she got stringy fibers in her mouth, but she kept at the task and finally accomplished it. Rejoicing but making all haste—for they must be nearly done eating by now—she bent to find the knots at her ankles.

As she was fumbling with these in the darkness, she grew aware of a new voice outside.

"...a young gentleman in green coat, light brown breeches, vest with...what's the word?...stripes. He stands this tall, the hair very dark, no beard...You have seen him?"

Count Modrowski! He had come after her—he must have seen the broken gig just in time—and keeping the secret of her disguise, too!

"Nay, ain't seen tetch nor trace on 'im," the crone was saying with a cackle.

Legs still bound, Viola rolled and scrabbled to the front of the caravan and snatched up the curtain. "Count! Count Modrowski!"

He was standing beside the fire with the gypsies, holding his horse. He took one look at Viola, turned, and punched the nearest gypsy full in the face.

The man—it was the big Gonzar—staggered back, touched his upper lip, and observed that blood was flowing from his nose. "Damn your impertinence, sir, what are you doing?"

"I have tapped your claret," the count said happily.

"Ah? Then I shall tap yours!"

The younger gypsy woman jumped to her feet and got between them. "Stop this! This is—undignified!"

Modrowski would have ignored her and taken them all on, if necessary, but Gonzar's voice and the woman's had told Viola everything. "It's all right, Count, it's all right! They *are* my own people in masquerade! It's all

183

right, they're friends!" And she gave a long laugh of pure relief.

"Masquerade?" said Modrowski.

Grumsen-Noddy Duncton clapped him on the back. "Aie, sir, masquerade, and damme if you ain't won my bet for me! Sir, I'd like to shake your hand."

Chapter 20.

Miss Merriweather had to admit that, although the rising tones in Beale's voice when she stepped between the two men would have counted as a clear sign of agitation, Spottiswood had flustered first. "But it took a Polander t' do it," she added as she gave Noddy her I.O.U. later that night in the Graham Arms. "And the Beale did crack the next minute after."

"Yes, ma'am, and no doubt that's a great comfort to you," Duncton replied.

"And what'll you do with my twenty-five hundred, eh?"

"Present them to the admirable Count Modrowski as a wedding gift, lest the sudden access of lucre corrupt me," said Duncton as if he had not money of his own equal to Miss Merriweather's.

Miss Ayrsford and Count Modrowski were enjoying a late supper, with Sebastian and Hector in the same private parlor as a sop to propriety; but Hector was contriving pretty well to occupy his friend's attention with an argument about who had been most to blame for alienating the captain and Sir Toby before the two young men had had a chance to meet the charming Miss Markham.

"And you will be my Countess Modrowska?" the count asked Viola under cover of the young men's raised voices.

"Modrowska? Oh, it's like the Latin, isn't it, with different endings for male and female."

"If it will be more English to say Countess Modrowski..."

"Not at all, I think Modrowska is delightful, and the other would probably sound outlandish to you. We'll return to London for the Little Season every year, of course, and for at least part of the great one."

"Every year," he promised. "And at Bluebriar you will go about in breeches and be masquerade Modrowski."

"And in London I shall go in skirts and be the Countess Modrowska and the envy of everyone."

Sebastian was half shouting "And they already had her good as engaged to Standeven, so what good would it have done you?"

Viola leaned over and snatched a kiss from her count.

Lord Spottiswood and Mrs. Beale were standing in the upstairs passage between their bedrooms. "Well, madam," he said, "the Markham party should be comfortable at a Carlisle inn by now."

"I should not be surprised if Alice's father and grandfather were to press for a marriage by license, though there is no reason they should not wait to have the banns published."

"Viola's marriage will proceed with all seemly leisure. I believe she has already expressed her preference for a large London wedding."

"I am not completely without hope that a reconciliation with the Markham family may be effected in time to arrange a double wedding," said Mrs. Beale. "But perhaps Alice and Mr. Standeven would prefer a small, rural ceremony in any case."

"It seems a pity," said Lord Spottiswood, "to arrive within five miles and return with no advantage had of Gretna Green."

"It seems a very great pity, sir."

"Your landaulet, for instance, could easily carry two over the Border tonight."

"Would the village blacksmith be prepared to conduct the ceremony in the middle of the night?"

"If he were not," said his lordship, "the hypothetical runaways could wait for morning and return here tomorrow."

"Or the day after," she agreed.

"For myself, madam, I find the events of the day have left my nerves at too high a pitch for repose to come quickly," he remarked with all his old composure. "What would you say to shocking society in general with me?" He offered her his elbow.

She accepted it. "I would say, sir, that I think I should rather enjoy a certain measure of mild notoriety."

Arm in arm, they slipped down a back way to the stables.

Lord and Lady Spottiswood did not return to Longtown until the middle of the following afternoon, which was rainy. By that time the others, not being blessed with an all but imperturbable temper, were somewhat on edge. Noddy Duncton and Miss Merriweather had insisted the missing pair could very well look to themselves, and were beguiling the wait with small bets on when and in what state the new runaways would get back. Viola added a few crowns to the betting and found pleasant enough devices to pass the time with her count, but perhaps Merriweather and Duncton should have let Sebastian and Hector chase off after their elders despite the foul weather and the implied disrespect. As it was, the two young men were in by far the worst seethe of the party, having spent the day in hotter and hotter argument on last night's bone of contention and any other subject for debate that fell in their way. Chess having proved beyond their powers of concentration, they were bickering over draughts, and the emotions of their weeks together in the Lake District—Hector's boredom there and Sebastian's annoyance at his friend's teasing—were now so mixed with more recent tensions that the return of the bridal couple rather exacerbated than quieted the lads' grievances.

Duncton, Miss Merriweather, and Viola were settling their little bets at one side of the common room, with Count Modrowski looking on, when Hector's voice rose loud enough for everyone to hear.

"Well, I never said I might want to *marry* Miss Markham, but I suppose a fellow don't have to propose to every young woman he meets?"

"And you were the one who mulled our chances, drawing us all into that preposterous gypsy business—"

"Well, it taught your sister a better lesson than any birch, didn't it? Why didn't you just desert us and go with Markham? You two blue-devil Puritans could have got on swimmingly together."

All Sebastian's resentment swelled, rose, and thundered down like a foaming breaker, and he flung a draughtman. It glanced off Hector's forehead, and that young man was only too ready for the excuse. Next instant they were locked together in a rough and tumble that carried them out the room and across the passage.

Wrestling and pommeling each other like puppies, with Viola and Modrowski trying to separate them and atching stray bruises from the flailing fists and heels for their pains, they burst into the private parlor where Lord Spottiswood and the former Mrs. Beale were taking tea after their excursion.

Noting that the struggle was likely to crash into the tea table, Lord and Lady Spottiswood lifted their teacups. As Hector and Sebastian rolled against the table and sent it toppling, Spottiswood raised an eyebrow at his bride. She raised one back, the corners of their mouths twitched slightly, and they put their cups to their lips, exchanging an unruffled gaze over the rims.